RED DIRT TRACKS

The Forgotten Heroes of Early Stockcar Racing

Gail Cauble Gurley

PublishAmerica
Baltimore

© 2005 by Gail Cauble Gurley.
All rights reserved. No part of this book may be reproduced, stored in a retrieval system or transmitted in any form or by any means without the prior written permission of the publishers, except by a reviewer who may quote brief passages in a review to be printed in a newspaper, magazine or journal.

First printing

ISBN: 1-4137-7992-1
PUBLISHED BY PUBLISHAMERICA, LLLP
www.publishamerica.com
Baltimore

Printed in the United States of America

In loving memory of my parents, Grayson and Vera Lingle Cauble; my grandmother, Minnie F. Lingle.

In honor of my husband, Ed; our daughter, Denise; our grandchildren, Charlie, Spencer and Madison. I love you all.

SPECIAL ACKNOWLEDGMENT:

Special thanks is given to Mike Sykes for his undying devotion and dedication to the old-time racers, car owners, mechanics, media, and racing officials by establishing and operating the Racing Legends Foundation, a non-profit organization established to provide financial assistance, especially for medical issues, to these people. Tax-deductible donations may be made to:

Mike Sykes
Racing Legends Foundation
119 Northeast Drive
Archdale, N. C. 27262

Gratitude and love to the Lewallen family for their support, encouragement and contributions in making this work possible. Also to my good friend and fellow writer, Pam Cable, for her unselfish encouragement and positive reinforcement of my work.

Online link at: www.racing-reference.com provided invaluable information regarding dates and stats.

Special thanks to the following for their sharing of information and memories that contributed to this book:

Robert and Marie Nooe
Fred and Betty Harb
Peewee and Shirley Jones
Billy Biscoe
Bill Blair Jr.
Mike Sykes
Carrie Lewallen
Rita Lewallen Walker
Gary Lewallen
Ned Jarrett

Red Dirt Tracks is a fictional drama based on historical events, real people and actual happenings about the lives and careers of early race car drivers, before and immediately following the advent of NASCAR. Information contained herein was gathered from family members, friends, or the drivers themselves, and is recorded as accurately as possible. Some names, characters, locations, and incidents portrayed are either the product of the author's interpretation, the memories of individuals reporting, or are used for effect. The literary perceptions and insights are based on experiences of family members, friends, or drivers, but some names, characters, places and incidents are either products of the author's imagination and perception or are used as combinations of incidents and characters for effect.

Dialog is added for effect, and as an effort to capture the essence and heart of these early drivers as presented by those who knew and loved them. It is not presented to be wholly accurate, word for word, as conversations conducted years ago cannot be remembered that way. Their essence, however, is presented with great respect and sensitivity in an effort to pay homage to their lives.

The information herein is true and as complete as possible based on interviews and research. All information is given without any guarantee on the part of the author or publisher. The author and publisher disclaim any liability incurred in connection with this data or specific details.

Any trademarked names, words, or model names are used in this book for identification purposes only. This is not an official publication approved or even acknowledged by NASCAR or any other trademarked source.

Reviews

Gail Gurley's entertaining writing style captures the spirit of the early pioneers in the race car business before it became the huge industry it is today. *Red Dirt Tracks* relates the early days of racing in a unique, enjoyable, and entertaining down-to-earth manner.
 Phillip J. Kirk, Jr., President and Secretary
 North Carolina Citizens for Business and Industry
 Publisher, NORTH CAROLINA Magazine

 Gail Gurley has done a wonderful job depicting the people in this book (both fictional and non-fictional) as true Americana. I felt totally comfortable with what she has written. She went beyond the "call of duty" in meeting drivers that are still living to capture their views and stories. She truly captured the spirit of these pioneers of racing. I appreciate her.
 Gary E. Lewallen, son of racing great, Jimmie Lewallen

Foreword

Since the beginning of recorded history, and very probably before that, man has engaged in racing and competition to determine the strongest, the fastest, the smartest, the best among a group. Men have raced on every mode of transportation ever developed including foot racing, horses, chariots, carriages, covered wagons, bicycles, motorcycles, boats, airplanes and the automobile. In their quest to defeat and win, bigger and stronger and faster machines are built, ever pushing the limits of human endurance and mechanical durability.

This is the story of the men, and a few women, who blazed the trail of automobile racing in what would become known as stock car racing. It chronicles their passion, dedication, determination and even obsession to participate in that which they loved so well–determining who had the fastest vehicle, the best control and who was the best driver. Speed had no meaning without control. Winning had no joy without honor. It was a contest of man and machine against man and machine. The two became one entity, one well oiled instrument of competition. Ten vehicles and ten drivers on a track became not twenty separate entities but ten purpose-driven, guided missiles with one goal – to reach the finish line first.

Most were honorable drivers who subscribed to fairness and justice, winning with integrity and fair play. The ones who didn't soon became outcasts, and with one or two exceptions, were left by the wayside, never to be remembered or thought of again. They were erased from the minds and memories of those who loved the sport so well, and were considered to be rogues and scalawags.

These early drivers laid the foundation of an accidental empire. There were no conscious plans or thoughts given to developing what would become the world's largest dynasty of organized stock car racing. Their talent and passion were too intense not to be recognized on a grand scale; thus, the organization evolved, much to the surprise of many drivers, business leaders and even the founding fathers of organized stock car racing.

This is the story of their accomplishments captured through the memories of their families or even the drivers themselves, from the ones who remain alive and spoke to the author. It is a chronicle of their sacrifices, their failures, their victories, their losses, their fears, superstitions and even paranoia as they bravely forged into unknown, uncharted and, sometimes, illegal and dangerous territory. They are classic examples of the American citizen, daring to go where no other has gone, eager to blaze new trails, undeterred by the fear of what danger or failure lie ahead.

Buck, Tommy and Mary Mason are fictional characters. In talking with these gentle giants of racing, there was one theme running through their thoughts and memories. They had certain superstitions and suspicions and fears. Some of those centered on the fear of being cheated of an earned victory through accident, technicality or downright deceit. The Mason fictional characters personify the fears and suspicions of these drivers. It is the age-old battle of good against evil, right against wrong. Evil sometimes won, but good prevailed. These magnificent men and women are the backbone of our nation's strength. Give them a simple piece of machinery and they see destiny and glory. These same people are the ones who will willingly go into battle to fight for that which our nation values so much – our freedom and our liberty to achieve and excel.

This is a story of races won and races lost, loves won and loves lost, of triumphs and failures, both on the racetrack and off. They lived and loved, and dreamed more intensely and passionately than most of us, and they dared to reach for their dreams, to take control of their destiny regardless of the criticism, the dangers or the consequences. They were, and are, real and genuine, human with virtues and faults, defects and commitment. They are complex, yet simple; conforming, yet defiant; suspicious, yet trusting.

Had they known they would have been denied and betrayed by the very sport they built, would they have begun their quest? Absolutely. These people who dared to achieve, who dared to conquer, who dared to dare, are our strength and encouragement. They try, they lose, they fail, they try again. They win, they rejoice, they try again. They emulate the American spirit and fervor. For the sport of racing is implanted onto their very souls.

This is their story- warts, wings and all.

CHAPTER 1
Jimmie Lewallen, Fred Harb, Bill Blair

Another bright May Sunday in High Point, North Carolina meant that soon many young men who owned cars, or had access to the family car, would be leaving church, and rushing to the racetrack to challenge their friends and test their vehicles. The large, oak doors of Springfield Friends Meeting burst open, allowing the hot sunshine to rush into the cool, dark entry.

The year was 1938, and young Jimmie ran through the doors, barely slowing down long enough to shake the minister's hand, poised in the doorway to greet his departing parishioners.

Jimmie jumped over the two entrance steps, pulling off his jacket and ripping off his tie as he ran.

"Jimmie! Jimmie Lewallen!"

He stopped several feet into the yard, removed his fedora, and turned toward his mama.

"Yes, ma'am?" he asked politely. His Southern upbringing had instilled a deep respect for his elders, especially his parents. This training would stay with him, as well as most of his peers, for a lifetime.

"You be careful on that racetrack, you hear? Don't you go getting hurt, and don't get in no fights."

"Yes, ma'am, I won't. I mean, I will." Jimmie turned and ran eagerly to his shiny, black 1936 Ford coupe parked by the driveway in the churchyard, tossed his coat, hat and tie into the back seat, rolled the sleeves of his white shirt up and slid behind the wheel. He smiled to himself as his hands caressed the steering wheel, warmed by the sun.

Beads of sweat glistened on his forehead and upper lip. Moist half moons stained his underarms as he thrust the key into the ignition and pushed the starter button. The engine roared to life and his heart raced as he became one with the throbbing, vibrating motor. The eager young racer revved the engine several times, basking in the power beneath his feet, pushed the clutch in, moved the stick shift to reverse. He let out the clutch, backed up, and pushed it into first, spinning gleefully down the driveway, rocks and dust scattering. Two young boys, about eight or nine-years-old, ran screaming and waving behind his car. His arm came out the side window, waving to them as they ran.

Jimmie's mother stood at the top of the steps, shaking her head and clicking her tongue. The other church members, some of them frowning, stood quietly on the steps, waiting for the young racer to make his dramatic exit. Several women held their squirming young in tow as they struggled to chase after the car with their two friends. A few managed to escape their mothers' grasps and raced after the car, squealing and waving their arms in delight and excitement. Jimmie glanced into the rearview mirror, laughing at their enthusiasm, then disappeared down the red dirt road.

As he approached Main Street, a two-lane ribbon paved street through the center of town, made a quick right turn, the rear end fishtailing, he changed gears and accelerated. He sped up Main Street, secure in the knowledge that the police department would not be out on the streets on a Sunday morning. Each intersection was checked in hopes of finding a challenger so he could practice and warm up his car for the upcoming race at High Point Speedway.

Jimmie approached the traffic signal at Lexington Avenue and stopped for the red light. A glance to his left revealed Bill Blair driving up to the light and turning left onto Main Street, on his way to the racetrack as well. Jimmie glanced both ways, saw no traffic approaching, and sped through the intersection under the still-red light. He pulled up behind Bill, next to his back bumper, nearly nudging it, waited impatiently for an oncoming car to meet and pass them, then jerked the car into the wrong lane, pulling up beside Blair's 1935 Ford. Jimmie waved, pointed forward, and the challenge was accepted.

The engines roared as they changed gears and accelerated, each vying for the lead, but not too quickly. They were testing the other vehicle and enjoying the thrill of cat and mouse. Several blocks up, an oncoming car pulled into the ditch to avoid being hit by Jimmie. Bill pulled over to the right, nearly getting in the ditch on his side of the street, so that Jimmie could avoid hitting the car head-on.

As they roared past the frightened driver, Jimmie glanced into his rearview mirror. The driver of the vehicle in the ditch exited and raised his fist in anger, yelling inaudible words in the direction of the two speeding vehicles. Jimmie laughed and then accelerated to pass Bill.

Jimmie passed Bill, though not without a struggle, and pulled out ahead so as to put distance between them. Several other cars meeting them denied Bill the opportunity to challenge his friend again. Churches were letting out and people were going home so their racing would have to wait until they got to the racetrack.

They screeched into the High Point Racetrack off the unpaved Johnson Street, pulling into the grassy area surrounding the red dirt track. They were followed and soon overtaken by the cloud of dust they created in their wake. Jimmie gunned the engine, turned the steering wheel, and made a full circle, throwing up pieces of dirt and grass. Their adrenalin was pumping, their young blood racing, and they were eager to start. About a dozen spectators stood on the sidelines by the one-mile circular track, their arms crossed, waiting for the games to begin. Some had buckets turned upside down to sit on, others just stood, too excited and anxious to sit.

The trees surrounding the track behind the wooden fence guarding the course were filled with people, mostly children. Unable to pay the ten-cent admission fee, they nonetheless wanted to see the action. The owner of the track yelled obscenities in their direction and hurled a dirt clod at a young boy sitting on a low branch. The child simply dodged the clod and remained there, undeterred by the aggression. He was impassioned with the prospect of seeing these young gladiators race around a track and was willing to risk being hit by a dirt clod, or even a rock, to watch them race. And the cussing didn't even faze him.

The cars had no seat belts but drivers were required to tie themselves in and tie their doors shut somehow. Most used belts or ropes and the only helmets they had were either WW I helmets belonging to their fathers or grandfathers or football helmets they used in school.

There were eight drivers racing on this particular Sunday afternoon. They took turns tearing around the track one at a time to see who would start first. Everyone qualified, but the lineup was based on how quickly each finished his circle. There were no stopwatches, so a volunteer with a second hand on his watch would time them.

Soon all the cars had run the track and were nearly ready to race. Jimmie Lewallen would start first with Bill Blair second and Fred Harb third. Fred had driven in from Greensboro and had missed the main street drag racing on the way to the track.

As they got ready to line up, two drivers near the back got in an argument.

"I know damn well my time was better than yours!" yelled one.

"Hell, man, you're crazy. I ran a whole bunch better than you did!"

The first one shoved the second, the second shoved back.

"I'll beat your ass, you stupid son-of-a-bitch," the first threatened.

"You ain't man enough to beat nobody's ass, jerk!"

Other drivers came running as fists began to fly. Soon they were all in a bunch, pushing and shoving and trying to break up the fight. A sudden scream from the other side of the fence caused them all to stop momentarily and look in that direction.

"He fell out of the tree!" A young man was screaming from high in a tree, pointing down to the ground. He was scrambling, trying to get down. "My brother fell out of the tree!"

All the racers and spectators ran to the fence, struggling to peer over to see if the young boy who had fallen was badly hurt. As they yelled and tried to crawl over the fence to help, the young victim ran to the base of the tree, brushed himself off and began to slowly climb back up to his vantage point.

"He's alright. You alright, boy?"

"Yeah, he's alright. Let's race!"

Soon the cars were running around the one-mile dirt track, sliding, skidding, and throwing rocks and dust. The race was three times around the track with the first one coming in declared the winner. Volunteers on the side kept up with how many times a particular car ran around the track. Some of the wives would keep score, and for the single ones they had brothers or buddies to do it.

Halfway around the second time, Fred Harb bumped into Bill Blair's back bumper. It spun Bill out and he slid into the center of the circle. He regained control and flew after Fred, madder than a hornet. He cut in front of Fred, causing him to slide sideways to a stop. While the dust was still swirling and cars were roaring by, Bill jumped out of his car, ran to Fred's side window and started cussing and punching him inside the car. Other cars on the track quickly stopped, as it was an unwritten rule to stop when there was a fight on the track.

"What the hell you trying to do, Fred? Kill me?" Bill was punching at Fred, trying to make a good connection to his face as Fred bobbed his head around and held up his arms in defense. Fred managed to get the belt off holding him in the car, crawled out the open window and knocked Bill off balance. He came toward Bill swinging.

They rolled around in the dust, neither of them making a good connection on the other. The most damage done was to their white shirts they had worn to church. The other drivers arrived and pulled them apart.

"Hey, fellas, wait until after the race to fight," Jimmie ordered. "Can't nobody race if you're gonna be rolling around all over the track like this."

They stood there glaring at each other, dirt and dust streaking down their faces and covering their shirts. One knee of Bill's trousers was torn. He looked down, saw the tear and whined, "My wife's gonna kill me for this."

Fred looked down at the small tear and said, "Ah, it ain't so bad. Come by my house after the race and Ma'll fix it for you."

They grinned at each other and returned to their cars. The spectators and scorers returned to their spots and the race resumed. In a few minutes, Jimmie Lewallen crossed the finish line first. A white handkerchief fluttering in the hand of the racetrack owner declared him the winner. After waving the "flag," the owner wiped the red dust off his face and stuck it back in his pocket. Spectators and scorers and other racers came running to congratulate the winner, while people in the trees yelled and screamed their appreciation.

In 1938, that was the only award a winner received. There was no prize money, no trophies, no newspaper reporters, and no TV cameras since there was no TV in 1938. They simply enjoyed racing; their only trophy: the thick, red dust clinging to the sweat of their brows, arms and the folds and creases of their clothing. It was difficult to imagine that the shirts they wore, now streaked and marked by red dust clinging to the folds, creases and body sweat, had once been white.

These young men raced because they loved it. It was in their blood, it was what they longed to do. Nobody had ever even thought about a sponsor or even a race car. They used their own personal cars and hoped and prayed they didn't tear them up. Especially the ones using the family cars. Young men borrowing the family car dreaded the thought of tearing it up and having to face their daddies with what they had done. The cars were not built to withstand the torture of sustained high speed and constant short turning. Axles would break, causing them to turn over and many parts of these early vehicles would break. Money was scarce and cars were hard to come by. There was no insurance and if somebody tore up a car, it was just gone. The thrill was just in challenging each other and answering that challenge.

Many young men had endured the pain and shame of having to face their fathers with the news that the prized family car was laying in a crumpled heap on some racetrack. And some had been pulled out of school and put to work in the local cotton mills to pay for these destroyed vehicles. Others had difficulty sitting down for several days after coming in contact with the business end of their daddy's leather belts. These punishments, however, did not deter them nor negate their determination to race and hopefully win. Even if they didn't win, they wanted to race. Winning was nice, but the thrill of running was the real reward.

They lined up for the second race in the order they had finished the first one. Jimmie was first and Bill and Fred were third and fourth. They finished the first lap and as they came around for the second lap, Fred noticed something lying in the middle of the track up ahead. He leaned forward, straining to see through the dust.

That's somebody's gas tank, he thought. *Hell, I'll fix him. He won't be able to put that thing back on and race no more today. I'll put him out of business for sure.*

He lined his car up with the tank and as he reached it, he ran over it with both his front and back wheels. He laughed as he looked into the rearview mirror and saw it laying, twisted, bent and destroyed, rocking back and forth in the middle of the track. As he turned his attention to the track in front of him, he suddenly lost power. The engine sputtered and the car slowed down dramatically.

"What the hell?" he muttered. He managed to pull to the inside of the circle to get out of the way, crawled out of his car, opened the hood and looked inside. Nothing looked out of place. He walked around and began to look under his car. That's when he noticed his gas tank was missing. The gas tank had come off on the first lap and there was enough gas to get back around to it. That was his own gas tank lying crumpled up on the ground, putting him out of the race for the day.

"Damn," he hissed. He kicked the ground and tossed his helmet through the windshield of his car. He stood there, looking helplessly at his own stupidity, trying to figure out what he was going to say to his daddy. He was driving the family car.

Fred was the first out that day, after running over his gas tank. Bill and Jimmie were running very well. One by one the drivers dropped out of the race. They either had mechanical trouble or a flat tire, or ran out of gas.

Tom Miller and Doug Davis, two sometime drivers, had been fighting before the race, each believing they had made better time than the other in qualifying. Tom had a flat tire before he got around the track for the second lap in the first race. There were no pit crews, so if a driver had no spare he was automatically out of the race. Drivers changed their own tires after a flat, but were almost always out of the current race while performing this work. They participated in the next race if they were quick enough in getting the tire on to replace the flat. Tom had no spare so he was just out of the race. Doug hit a deep rut as he ran off one side of the track, jerked the wheel and felt the unmistakable jolt of a broken axle. He slipped carefully out of his car, kicked the back tire and walked dejectedly off the track and out of the way.

"Guess it don't really matter none which of us was fastest in qualifying," Doug commented as he stood beside Tom.

"Guess you're right. What happened?"

"Broke my axle. And this here's my pop's car. Don't know what I'm gonna tell him when I get home. He uses this car to get to work everyday."

"Yeah, I know what you mean. That's my dad's car too, and he ain't got no spare. Guess I'll try to get it fixed soon as the race is over."

The two stood silently, worried frowns on their faces.

The event was called when the competitors were down to two drivers. Jimmie and Bill were the only racers left. All the spectators and other drivers yelled their anger at the race being stopped and demanded that a final race be run between these two popular drivers.

"Naw, naw, that ain't right!" yelled one spectator. "Let 'em run against each other. We want a real winner!"

The official, who also happened to be the racetrack owner, relented and Jimmie Lewallen and Bill Blair prepared to race. The crowd was standing in anticipation, leaning forward in their eagerness, and several men reached into their pockets to make wagers on their favorite. The crowd was strangely quiet, even the spectators in the trees were silent, hanging onto limbs as they leaned over from their precarious perches, straining to get closer to the action.

The dust-stained handkerchief dropped and they were off. The crowd exploded in cheers and excitement, some of them running along side the track in an attempt to chase the speeding vehicles. Several of the people in the trees stood up on their branches, clinging to smaller branches around them so as not to fall. The leaves were fluttering with the fervor of the people perched in their limbs.

They completed the first lap with Jimmie just a half bumper ahead. Bill pulled in very close to him in an attempt to intimidate him. Jimmie pushed the accelerator all the way to the floor, blew his horn to distract Bill, and pulled out front. He stayed in front of Bill, not allowing him to pass.

About halfway through the second lap, Bill pulled his car to the left in an attempt to pass Jimmie. He ran his left side tires off the dirt track onto the grass in the center. He floor boarded the accelerator, throwing clumps of grass and dirt and gravel far into the air. The crowd went wild as he pulled in front of Jimmie, nearly clipping his front bumper as he did. Jimmie jerked to the right to avoid contact and slid sideways down the track.

Spectators scattered in terror as the speeding car careened toward them, dust and rocks flying. Jimmie struggled with the steering wheel in a valiant effort to keep from overturning. He finally came to a standstill in the middle of the track, heading in the wrong direction. He managed to get the car turned around and took off with a vengeance to catch his adversary.

He saw Bill making the turn on the last half of the final lap. He cut across the grass in the middle of the track, bearing down on his competition. Bill saw him coming, increased his speed, pulled to the far right of the track and just managed to miss being struck as Jimmie bounced onto the track from the grass. It had ceased to be a race and had become a battle. The last few hundred feet were intense as the two bore down on each other, not even caring if they won or lost, just wanting to knock each other out. Bill crossed the finish line first by just a few inches. They both came to a screeching, sliding halt and were almost immediately out of their cars, fire in their eyes and anger in their hearts.

"You cut me off, you son-of-a-bitch!" Jimmie screamed.

"Hell, you're crazy, you ignorant jackass!" Bill screamed in return. "You wouldn't let me by. You're lucky I didn't kill you!"

Jimmie swung and connected on Bill's face with his huge fist, sending him sailing. Blood spurted from Bill's nose as he scrambled up, running as hard and fast as he could. He hit Jimmie full force, knocking him to the ground. They wrestled, and cussed and panted, rolling in the mud and the dust and the blood. Fred and several others finally got them pulled apart.

"Cut it out, you two!" Fred yelled. "There ain't no sense in this. Just cut it out!"

They stood there facing each other, angrily glaring, faces red and wet with sweat. Bill wiped the blood from his face with the back of his hand. They both attempted to brush the dust from their pants and shirts but it was a hopeless effort.

Bill was declared the winner but there was no prize money and no trophy. Just the jubilation and appreciation from the crowd. The fight was readily forgotten and Jimmie slapped his friend on the back, shaking his hand. Soon spectators and drivers were leaving. Several of the drivers stood looking in despair at their cars, trying to figure out how to get them home for needed repairs. There were no trailers or pit crews and mechanics to help them out. They were strictly on their own.

Bill, Jimmie and Fred gathered around Fred's wounded vehicle. The destroyed gas tank lay in the field beside the track and the broken windshield glared angrily at the trio.

"Now what the hell am I gonna do?" Fred wondered.

Jimmie turned and trotted to his car. He crawled in, started the engine and backed it up in front of Fred's car.

"Let's hook her up, and I'll haul you up to the shop and we'll try to get her fixed."

Fred worked in his father's garage in High Point and many nights and weekends, he and his friends would work on their cars up there.

Soon they arrived at the shop and Fred unlocked the bay. They pushed the car inside and set about getting the repairs done. There was a windshield still in the cardboard packaging, ready to be placed in a customer's vehicle the next day. Without hesitation, Fred pulled it over to his car, removed it from the cardboard and began to remove the damaged one from his car.

"Whatcha gonna tell your pop tomorrow?" Bill asked.

"Ain't gonna tell him nothing 'cause I don't know nothing. I'll call the company in the morning and order another, and I'll pay for it."

They all laughed and began to help Fred take the windshield out of his car. They loaded the broken windshield and the empty cardboard box into Bill's car so as to hide any evidence of what they had done.

"I'm gonna go on home and I'll dump this stuff on my way." Bill announced. "I don't want to be gone too long, what with Lucille being in the family way and all."

"Okay, Bill, many thanks for your help," Fred said. "Me and Jimmie'll get this windshield in and I'll put a new gas tank on. I still can't believe my luck."

They all stood quietly for a few seconds and then started laughing uncontrollably.

"Running over your own damned gas tank! That was rich," Jimmie laughed.

"Hell, I didn't know it was mine." Fred was laughing, but was embarrassed by his mistake. "Guess I had enough gas in the carburetor and the gas line to get another lap and a half around the track 'fore it ran out."

They were still chuckling as Bill turned to leave.

"Oh, by the way," he said as he reached his car, "there's a race down at the track in Pageland, South Carolina next weekend. Gonna be pretty big. Bill France is gonna be there."

"That'll be a good race. I guess Buck Mason'll be there too," Jimmie observed.

"Yeah, I'm sure of that," Fred lamented. "He ain't gonna miss no chance to take a race. Just watch your back."

"Hell, with him, you gotta watch everything! Y'all going?" Bill asked.

CHAPTER 2
Moonshine and Hard Driving

The drivers went about their normal duties during the week, eagerly anticipating Saturday's race in Pageland. They worked at their normal jobs, some at the local cotton mills, some delivering groceries, working at service stations or garages, or even attending classes at their local high schools.

Drivers from High Point gathered each night at the Harb Garage to work on their cars with Fred Harb supervising. He was a great mechanic as well as a generous benefactor, willingly offering advice and parts to anyone in need. He had the respect of all his peers, even the ones not privileged to know him personally. His reputation of giving a part or a spare tire to any racer at the racetrack was well documented. If you needed it and Fred had it, it was yours.

Most of them lived at home as single men. The only married one in the group was Bill Blair, and every dollar the single ones made went into improving, modifying and spiffing up their cars. They had very little interest in women, except as an occasional distraction, and concentrated on their racing. Their jobs were merely a means to an end, the end being having the parts and equipment needed to race their cars.

Jimmie had no job except running moonshine, so he managed to keep his car together and help his mother with what he earned in running this cash product. Fred worked at his dad's garage, earning a little money and having access to many auto parts for himself and his friends. He didn't give money to his parents, but his working at the garage helped his dad. Fred did great work and was well respected by customers bringing their vehicles in for service and repair.

The excitement and anxiety of these young men increased as the week trudged on. Most of them had decided to drive down to South Carolina on Friday night, spend the night in their cars, and be ready when the sun came up on Saturday morning. Their trips were like camp outings and all-night parties. Many of the drivers ran moonshine whiskey from the mountains of North Carolina (mostly Wilkes County), and would make their deliveries on the way to the track.

Jimmie Lewallen turned off onto a dirt road just inside the state of South Carolina to make his whiskey delivery. Fred Harb drove on by, blowing his horn in salute to his friend. Fred had never run moonshine. He didn't condemn his friends for doing it, but he had no wish to make money in this way. People would sometimes get sick, or worse, after drinking some of the homemade spirits that had been filtered through lead radiators. It could be a dangerous liquid. Besides, Fred was fortunate to be able to support his racing habit by working with his dad.

He arrived at the racetrack just before dark and soon had a campfire going. Other friends and drivers began to arrive and gathered around the fire, greeting, smiling and laughing, just glad to be together. Fred was relieved to see Jimmie arrive at the campsite safely just after dark.

"Jimmie." Fred nodded his head in greeting, but made no further comment.

Jimmie grinned back at his friend, knowing that Fred worried about his running the illegal load. Jimmie did what he had to do in order to help his mother and keep his race car running.

The men sat at the track all night, talking and lying, and laughing and drinking moonshine whiskey or beer until the sun began to poke away at the night sky. A quick nap before the races started was all they needed. Their youth and adrenalin kept them prepared for the battle on the racetrack. The moonshine was clear and left no hangover headache, just an occasional case of vomiting and dry mouth.

These bulky, heavy cars were extremely difficult to drive as they lacked power steering or power brakes. It was a battle driving them, even without worrying about trying to control them in spin outs and turnarounds. A driver in these early cars could easily lose 20 pounds during a race. Their hands were frequently bloody and bruised at the end of the run, the result of fighting the steering wheel through the ruts in the dirt tracks and around the curves.

Fred Harb buckled up, using an Army pistol belt his father wore in WW I. He was driving a 1934 Ford convertible with no roll bars on it. Bill Blair had arrived just before dawn that morning, ready to race. He was under the hood, giving his car a final once-over before race time. Jimmie Lewallen sat behind the wheel of his car, testing the accelerator and listening for any suspicious engine noises. It was purring like a kitten. He smiled to himself, wiping a bit of dust off the steering column.

Bob Welborn was tinkering under his hood, making last minute checks and actually wasting time. He had checked and re-checked every part and wire under the hood. He wiped at imaginary grease and oil on the spotless motor, and closed the hood lovingly.

The four friends generally wound up close to each other at every track. They sought each other out and drew comfort and security from the presence of each.

"How's she running?" Fred approached Jimmie's car.

"Sounds real smooth," Jimmie bragged, obvious relief in his voice.

"That new carburetor we put on the other night must have been the ticket." Bill leaned down, pulling up the hood of Jimmie's car as he spoke. The friends had worked long and hard on all three cars during the week.

"Yep, and I appreciate you helping me out with that, fellows. I owe you one."

"You owe us a bunch, friend," Bill laughed. "But we ain't keeping no score card or nothing."

"Just the same, I got a extra spare tire if one of you need it during the race. Just let me know."

"I reckon you'll know alright, if we need one," Fred observed.

They laughed and stood around, tinkering with the valves and wires and spark plugs, having nothing to do but just enjoying each other's company and the thrill of the upcoming race.

"Has everybody got a jack?" Bob questioned. He knew they did, but making small talk before a race gave them all comfort.

"If you ain't got one, I can rent you one. I got an extra."

They turned to the voice coming from their right and scowled at Buck Mason.

"Hell, Buck," Jimmie accused, "you'd sell oxygen to your dying mama."

The others laughed and Buck snorted at them, turned and stomped away.

They reported to the starting line, one at a time, for

qualifying. Qualifying meant driving once around the track and the fastest one started in front. There were 12 cars on the track that day. The race was to start at 10:00, and by 8:30 spectators were lining up outside the wooden gate blocking the drive. There was no fence but just a gate so that the owner of the track could sell tickets. The cars were parked outside the track and many people would just walk right into the track area without going through the gate. The owner employed local deputies to catch as many of them as possible, and several spectators would come in contact with the unfriendly end of a nightstick before the start of a race. The quarter-mile track surrounded a shallow lake and makeshift bleachers stood precariously around the outside of the track. Many people sat or stood on the ground, or sat on wooden boxes brought along. A few of the bleachers were leaning to one side, both from age as well as being hit by runaway race cars and being shoddily repaired. Few people wanted to run the risk of sitting on them unless they sat on the bottom level. The two higher ones weren't too secure and were too difficult to escape quickly.

Some of the spectators backed their cars up to the edge of the racetrack and sat on bumpers or trunks. This, too, was dangerous as an-out-of-control, runaway car leaving the track could take out anything and everything, or everybody in its path.

The drivers lined up after their qualifying and got ready to race. Buren Skeen was third behind Jimmy Pardue, and Fred Harb was behind Buren. Jimmie Lewallen was sixth in the lineup and Bill Blair was second.

The lap counters sat on the side, their pencils poised above their notepads, nervously keeping an eye on their particular driver. Most of them were cousins or brothers, or friends of the drivers and since all the cars were black, it was difficult to tell them apart. A few of the drivers had tied different colored ribbons to their radio antennas perched on the front side of the car at the passenger door in an attempt to make them more visible. However, the dust stirred up along with the general confusion of speed and excitement frequently caused the tiny ribbons to disappear from view.

The white handkerchief dropped and they were off. A cloud of dust and spinning dirt engulfed the screaming, jumping crowd as the cars struggled to find their position. At the end of a race, the spectators would be as dusty as the drivers. After removing goggles or sunglasses, the drivers and spectators looked like a large group of raccoons, their eyes the only thing clean in a face and body covered with red dust.

The faster cars quickly streaked by the others, leaving even more dust and dirt in their wake. Drivers, wearing various helmets from old WW I styles rescued from garages and attics, to football helmets kept as souvenirs from high school, fought to pass and head the pack.

Fred's car was faster than Buren's, but Buren was weaving back and forth in front of Fred to keep him from passing. Each time Fred steered to the right, Buren would pull in front of him. He'd steer to the left and Buren would steer to the left. Fred steered right to draw Buren and then jerked the steering wheel to the left. Buren lost control and slid sideways across the track, forcing Fred off the track. Spectators around the pond scurried away, and two of them jumped into the water in their eagerness to escape.

Fred managed to regain control without running into the water or turning over and came to a halt back on the track. He jumped from his car and made a mad dash for Buren, fire in his eye. Buren was attempting to get his car turned back into the proper position when suddenly, fists and arms and a head came tearing through his open window. Fists were flailing and he looked with surprise into the wild eyes of Fred Harb, pupils dilated with anger.

"What the hell?" he muttered, completely caught off guard.

"Are you crazy, you stupid son-of-a-bitch? What you trying to do, kill me?"

Tires were screeching around the two parked vehicles as other drivers stopped to avoid hitting them. Drivers were leaning out of their cars, shaking their fists and cussing the two blocking the track.

Fred was leaning into Buren's car, his feet off the ground, struggling to make contact with something that would hurt his adversary. Thanks to the helmet and ducking and dodging on Buren's part, little damage was done. Fred felt himself being pulled from the car and thrown rather unceremoniously to the ground, still sputtering and cussing and declaring his forever hatred for this driver who had made him so angry. He scrambled up, attempting to reach his enemy once more. Several arms held him back.

"Hold it, Fred! Just settle down," Bill France demanded.

Fred looked around and saw several of the drivers outside their cars while others hung out their windows, anxious to get this demonstration over so they could race. He kicked at the ground, muttering under his breath, tossing the look of death to Buren Skeen.

"Let's race!" he shouted, and ran to his car, threading himself through the open driver's side window, feet first. He wrapped the belt around his waist, and started the engine.

Buck had never left his car nor turned his engine off, waiting for a chance to get ahead of the leaders. He sped off in a cloud of dust, trailed by obscenities and gestures from the field.

The other drivers sprinted to their cars, quickly getting inside to start their engines. One driver actually leapt into his car headfirst, only to waste precious seconds getting himself turned around inside and buckled in. Soon they were racing around the track, the lap counters straining to keep up with their charges. Buren Skeen didn't get around Fred Harb again. Fred would later say that he won the race because he beat

Buren Skeen. It made little difference to him that Gwyn Staley took the win that day with Tiny Lund a close second. Fred felt he had won because Buren had lost.

Buck made his usual challenge to the win, but he had no sympathy or support from the sideline judges. He tried to say he finished a lap faster than he did, but the judges had already confiscated his score pad from his lap counter. He cussed his son out.

"Hell, I thought the least you could do was count," he accused the frightened boy. "Guess I was wrong. You ain't never gonna count for me again. I'll find someone with sense enough to count next time." He stormed off, leaving his son Tommy hurt and confused.

They were all standing around in a group after the race, discussing the turns and problems and near wrecks. Several had been knocked out of the race by mechanical problems but there had been no serious accidents. That in and of itself was a miracle, considering the fight that had occurred in the middle of the track between Fred and Buren. They were laughing about it, and even Fred gave Buren a reluctant smile when they heard a shout from the sidelines. They turned to see a car bumping over the grass, headed toward the racetrack. A man, obviously drunk, was leaning out the window, waving his arm and shouting.

"I'll show you hillbillies how to drive a damn race car!" he cried as he approached the track.

They stared in shock, their mouths open, as he reached the track and drove right straight across it into the pond in the center. His car was standing on its headlights, stuck in the mud. As they started running toward him, the driver tumbled out of the open window and into the muddy water, head first. His feet were suspended in the air for what seemed like a long time, but was actually only a second or two. His legs tumbled over and his head came up as he sat in the shallow water, sputtering and spitting, mud caked in his hair and on his face.

"What the hell happened?" he coughed, obviously stunned and confused but unhurt.

The crowd began to point and laugh uncontrollably at the sight. His family and friends soon arrived to pull their embarrassment out of the mud.

"Doug, you dumb fool, what the hell you trying to do?" one man yelled.

"I'm gonna show them how to race."

"Yeah, you showed 'em alright," he muttered as he pulled his buddy from the mud.

After the drivers got control of their laughter, they took off their shoes, waded into the water and pulled the car back down onto its wheels. They hooked a chain to the back bumper and pulled it out of the lake with another car.

Fred crawled under the hood and checked it out.

"It's a bit muddy but it'll be alright, I reckon. You might want to take some of that pond water after the mud settles a bit and wash it off under the hood, especially around the radiator. Be careful not to get no water in the carburetor and it should start okay." He was still chuckling as they all walked away.

Racing continued to grow in popularity, but the drivers barely noticed. They just wanted to race and go home, hopefully with at least a small purse, and live to race the next week. Some promoters would advertise a race, sell tickets and then leave with the prize money while the race was being run. Fewer and fewer unscrupulous promoters, however, would run away with the prize money as crowds of spectators became larger and more vocal.

After the usual controversy started by Buck at the end of one race, Gwyn and Tiny walked over to the ticket window to collect their first and second prize money. There was a commotion coming from the sidelines so they stopped to see what was happening now. It was something new and different every few minutes in some of these events. A crowd of men was holding a man captive. This was no easy task as the captive was kicking and screaming and cussing.

"Let me go, damn it! You got no right to hold me down. Let me go!"

"I got a sneaking suspicion who they might be holding onto," Tiny remarked, glancing over at Gwyn.

"Yeah, me too," Gwyn agreed.

They moved toward the crowd and sure enough, struggling to get free was the promoter, the one with their winnings. The crowd turned him loose as the two winners approached, but kept him surrounded so he couldn't get away should he take a notion to run.

"Where you going, Mr. Fraley?" Gwyn addressed the angry promoter.

"Ain't going no-damn-where! And these men got no business a-holding onto me neither!"

"I guess you got our winnings then," Tiny said.

"Yeah. They're right here." The promoter reached into his pocket and pulled out the $25 first prize and $10 second prize. He stuffed it in the waiting hands of Gwyn and Tiny, then turned and stormed off, still muttering and cussing under his breath.

"He was trying to get away," one of the men in the group explained.

"Yeah, that's kinda what we figured. We're much obliged to you folks for helping us out."

Some of the drivers were becoming well known, and Lee Petty was winning a number of races. He was a deliberate racer, determined to do it with seriousness and professionalism. He saw it as a valid way to make a living, and he was becoming a popular figure with the fans.

Drivers were a very suspicious and superstitious lot, careful not to breach what they viewed as a threat to their safety or luck. They had simple uniforms, usually just a white shirt with their name embroidered on it, and their name painted on their helmets. They had begun to paint numbers on their cars so that scorers could better track them. Drivers were very careful never to have a speck of green, as this was a taboo, on any of their uniforms or cars, not even their socks. This was the result of a long-ago fatality in the early 1940s involving a driver wearing green pants and driving a green car. As his broken body was removed from the wrecked car, someone pointed to his green pants.

"Hey, look at that. He's wearing green pants and driving a green car. That must be what brought him bad luck."

A taboo against the color green was born at that moment.

Peanut shells became another taboo after a rumor circulated that a brother of one of the drivers was eating peanuts around the race car before the race and somehow, shells had gotten into the gas tank. The car wrecked during the race, knocking the driver out of the race for the rest of the day. Therefore, peanuts joined the ranks of items to be avoided on the track. It's doubtful that peanut shells actually found their way into the gas tank, but there was no convincing the drivers of this. They took no chances and easily accepted any rumors regarding bad luck.

Bill France promoted several races himself and had one in South Carolina with a $500 purse promised to the winning driver. He tacked up signs all over town, slipped flyers in mailboxes, talked to local radio stations and knocked on doors for weeks. As the date of the race arrived, he became extremely uneasy. His promise of $500 was a great deal of money in that day and age, and he wasn't at all sure he'd sell enough tickets to raise that much. There was not so much concern about making a profit but he was afraid to face some of the very men he had raced with and against for so long.

As the crowd began to slowly trickle into the racetrack area, France became more and more nervous. Suddenly, he turned, nearly ran to his car and got inside. He started the engine, pulled away from the track and onto the highway. Bill gnawed away at his fingernails as he sped down the highway, anxious to put mileage between him and his angry friends.

What the hell am I doing? he thought. *I'm doing the very thing I've cussed so many others for doing. I can't betray these men. They're my buddies. Surely they'll understand if I can't make good my promise. And I'll get them later. I swear I will.*

He made a U-turn in the road, and drove back to the track. He nearly lost his courage a couple of times but his resolve was firm. He would not run out on his friends. When Bill arrived back at the racetrack, it was packed with spectators and the race was well underway. Total intake for the day was $782. Not only was the $500 purse paid but there was a $282 profit. Bill France was beginning to develop a glimmer of an idea. This could be a very profitable and lucrative business if handled correctly.

World War II came along and several drivers had their racing careers interrupted by military service, but they didn't forget their roots and their love of the race. Jimmie Lewallen joined the Army and spent four years in the European Theater of Operation under General George Patton's command. Jimmie distinguished himself many times during his military service, serving his country with the same dedication and devotion he put into all that he did. He was wounded twice, and was actually captured by the enemy on two separate occasions. However, he managed to escape both times and by the end of his four years service, Jimmie had been awarded the Bronze Star, Good Conduct Medal, American Defense Service Medal, American Campaign Medal, European-African-Middle Eastern Campaign Medal, and three Bronze Service Stars, along with the World War II Victory Medal and his Honorable Service Lapel Button.

Jimmie was in the assault at Normandy and was struggling to get onto the beach, out of the choppy waters of the ocean. He became genuinely frightened as he struggled; even more frightened than he was when he was the target of enemy fire. He could barely keep his head above water and was fearful that he was going to drown. *This would be a really crazy way to go out in a war,* he thought. As his head was covered by yet another large wave, he began to pray, *God, please get me out of this water alive. If you do, I promise I'll never get involved with any other water except to bathe and drink it.* Jimmie did survive that landing, but he never forgot his promise and never again entered the water. He would ride in a boat and travel on it but he would not swim. While lying in a foxhole in Europe during one of the many battles he encountered, he developed frostbite. Jimmie could not remember being so cold in all his life, and he would never forget how very cold the ground could be.

Shortly after being discharged from the Army, Jimmie and Carrie were married. He would sometimes talk to her about his experiences in the Army, and one of the most poignant stories he shared with her was his agony in that cold foxhole.

"If I die before you, Carrie, you make sure I'm good and dead before they put me in that cold ground. I don't never want to be that cold again."

Jimmie picked up his racing career shortly after returning from World War II. It was too dangerous running moonshine anymore so he quit that trade.

These early drivers thrived on driving around the Southeast, and even into Langhorne, Pa., to race. Promoters began to tack posters up on street signs, trees and telephone poles in the cities with racetracks, to advertise upcoming events. Notices were mailed to known drivers, and these drivers would in turn tell their friends and family. Some of the friends would participate in the races themselves while family members would travel to the site to watch the sport. Promoters awarded cash for winners so the fire of passion for winning was fanned. If the income generated by ticket sales didn't cover the promised prize as well as show a profit for the promoters, these unscrupulous promoters would disappear after the race started. This understandably angered the drivers, but it discouraged very few of them from racing. They would have done it for nothing, just for the thrill of the race and the chase.

Bill France was particularly angered by the behavior of some of these dishonest men. He began to watch these promoters very closely during a race, even recruiting some of the local lawmen to keep an eye on them. These racers were becoming folk heroes and the law eagerly helped them out anyway that they could. It became more and more difficult for promoters to abscond with the promised purses.

Jimmie and Carrie Lewallen had married in 1946, and Fred and Betty Harb married about the same time. They would all get together with the Bill Blair, Buck Mason, and Lee Petty families after the races, usually at the Lewallens' house, and socialize. Carrie, an excellent cook, always had a cake or special dish to share with the crowd. The children would play together, unaffected by the fame and attention their fathers were beginning to generate. It seemed that a new child came along to one of the families just about every year. The Harbs and Lewallens each eventually had three children.

When the families couldn't travel with their husbands, the women would get together and provide companionship and support of each other. They were together on just such an occasion as their husbands raced in Langhorne, Pa.

"Carrie, would you mind sharing that recipe for the coconut cake you fixed last weekend?" Betty Harb asked.

"Course you can have it, Betty!" Carrie exclaimed. "I'm proud to share it with you or anyone else that wants it."

"I'd like it, too," Lucille Blair commented as she picked Rita, the Lewallens firstborn, up off the floor. "Come on, Rita. I'll give you a bath. It'll soon be bedtime."

Carrie smiled her gratitude to her friend and retrieved the requested recipe from her kitchen drawer.

The drivers would phone home after each race, to let their wives know they were okay, and who won the race. Langhorne was quite a distance from Piedmont North Carolina, where Fred Harb, Bill Blair and Jimmie Lewallen lived. Precious coins had to be deposited in the pay phones after each race so as to advise the family that all was well.

Jimmie discovered that a certain size washer was just the exact size of a nickel and he would deposit these washers to complete a call home. Carrie sat anxiously by the phone after the time that she knew a race should end, waiting for the blessed ring that would relieve her anxiety. She had learned shortly after their marriage not to complain to Jimmie about his racing.

"Jimmie, I wish you wouldn't race. It dangerous and it scares me to death," she once complained.

"Hush, woman. You knew I raced when you married me,

so I don't want to hear it."

She hushed.

The men would chuckle at Jimmie's creativity in making his phone calls back home. His good friend, Bill Blair, was especially amused.

"Yeah, you're pretty slick, Lew. I think we oughta call you Langhorne Lew."

And so, Jimmie Lewallen became known throughout the racing circuit as Langhorne Lew.

The three were scheduled to race in Langhorne the following month, and Bill France and Bill Blair traveled to the radio stations in the Langhorne area, talking about the upcoming race. A particularly popular radio personality in Pennsylvania was Frank Smith. He worked at a country radio station in Langhorne, and would talk to France and Blair on the radio about upcoming races. The program reached all the way to the Piedmont area of North Carolina so people living there would make plans to travel to Langhorne on the date of the race. Smith would close out his program with, "Like the farmer told the potato: plant me now, dig me later." And people loved to hear him say that. He was very supportive of the Southern boys who loved to drive their cars like maniacs.

"Just want to remind all my listeners out there that the Rebel Rough Riders from the South are gonna be here in Langhorne next weekend to run a race. We'll have Pepper Cunningham, Johnny Goldblatt, Cliff Weathers, the Ferguson boys, Red Byron, Ed Samples, Billy Cardin, Red Hall, Bill Blair, Fred Harb and Jimmie Lewallen. These Rebel Rough

Riders are real hell raisers on the tracks up here and they'll put on a good show for you. Mark it down and be sure to be there. Gonna be a lot of fun.

"Well, like the farmer told the potato: plant me now, dig me later. I'll see you good folks next Saturday at the racetrack."

The public did not look as these men as drivers. They were seen as wild and crazy daredevils, and spectators were in awe of these men who would drive their cars at unheard of speeds, crashing into each other, fighting and cussing and scrapping, their hands bloody masses from fighting the steering wheels and each other. With no power steering, the cars were difficult to steer and even more difficult to control at high speeds. Local drivers were becoming bonified, qualified and certified heroes, and people didn't like strangers and outsiders coming into their towns and beating their hometown boys. These old-time tracks could be rough and unfriendly, especially to drivers not from that particular area.

Jimmie was driving a race for Bobby Myers in the 1950s at Creedmoor, N. C., near Durham. Earl Moss was the big star at Creedmoor. Before the race, Earl pulled Jimmie aside and warned, "Listen, Jimmie, if you win, drive by real quick and pick up your check, and then hightail it through the front gate."

Jimmie had been winning many races and was building up quite a reputation among the racing circuit, so Earl knew Jimmie had a good chance of winning at Creedmoor.

"Why?" Jimmie asked.

"Just trust me, buddy, and do it."

Jimmie won the race and tried to heed Earl's advice, but

people crossing the road in front of him slowed him down. As he sat there waiting to make his escape, a large, sweaty man approached his car. He arrived at Jimmie's window, and Jimmie began to feel somewhat uneasy.

"Hi, buddy, what can I do for you?" Jimmie asked nervously.

Without saying a word, the man reached under his shirt and pulled a .38 out of the front of his pants. He pointed it at Jimmie's head, and Jimmie prepared to duck. Suddenly another man appeared, grabbed the man holding the gun, and Jimmie made a hasty retreat.

The next week in Cornelius, Ga., Jimmie was preparing to run a race. Ed Samples was the king in Cornelius, and Ed gave Jimmie the same advice.

"If you win, Jimmie, pick up your money and get out in a hurry. People here don't like strangers coming in and beating local winners."

This time, the advice was heeded without question. Sure enough, Jimmie won. He barely escaped the angry mob running toward his car. He got out of the track and was quickly followed by three vehicles filled with angry fans. As Jimmie left the track, he saw a highway patrolman outside the track, standing beside his vehicle, directing traffic.

"I don't reckon I've ever been so glad to see a lawman in my life," Jimmie explained to the trooper.

"You must have won the race," the trooper observed. "Get on down the road and I'll hold these people here for awhile. That will give you a head start."

Jimmie never looked back.

Posters were nailed to telephone poles and doors and windows, advertising upcoming races. Any radio stations willing to listen to them were visited and Bill France would use this as their only source of advertising.

Bill Blair, Fred Harb and Jimmie Lewallen stuck together through the years and the fights, the triumphs and the failures. They were as close as any brothers and seemed to glean strength from the presence of each other. The three were at a track in Milwaukee for a 250-mile race one weekend. Bill France would schedule races around Detroit, as close as possible to that city, so that the car manufacturers would come out and watch. France was hoping to get them interested in becoming sponsors of the cars.

Blair and Lewallen shared a room at the hotel in Milwaukee that particular weekend. They were on the 12th floor of the building, and neither of them had ever seen a building this high before and certainly had never stayed in one. They ate their dinner in the lobby of the hotel and Bill seemed unusually quiet. Jimmie watched him but made no comment.

Guess he's got a lot on his mind, Jimmie worried.

When Bill finished eating, he stood up.

"Where you going?" Jimmie inquired.

"Back up to the room. I just wanta rest awhile. Sorta tired."

"Okay, I'll be up directly." Jimmie didn't voice his concern, but watched his friend as he walked to the elevator and entered to go upstairs.

In a few minutes, Jimmie went upstairs himself. He opened the door and started to step inside. When he did, he noticed Bill sitting on the ledge of the open window of the room, his feet hanging over into the open air. Jimmie quietly closed the door and ran to the stairs, unwilling to wait for the elevator. He soon arrived downstairs, breathless and frantic. The first person he saw was Hubert Westmoreland, the mechanic who worked on and cared for Bill's car.

Jimmie grabbed Hubert's arm and exclaimed, "Come on up here to our room, we gotta sneak up on him, he's fixing to jump!"

"Who?" Hubert asked with alarm. "What's the matter with you?"

"Come on! We gotta hurry. It's Blair, he's fixing to jump out the window!"

"What the hell?" Hubert jumped to his feet and ran quickly to the elevator with Jimmie.

Soon the two men stood in front of the door. They opened it quietly, and sure enough, there was Bill, still sitting on the windowsill, his feet dangling on the outside. He was leaning over, peering below him. They tiptoed up silently behind their friend and Jimmie grabbed Bill around the waist and pulled him back into the room, landing him unceremoniously on the floor.

"What in the hell are you doing, Lew? Are you crazy?" Bill sputtered.

"Well, you was fixing to jump and I couldn't let you do that."

"Naw, I wasn't gonna jump, I was just airing out my feet and watching them people way down there on the ground. They look like ants."

Jimmie was embarrassed by his behavior, and took much good-natured ribbing from the other drivers when the story was shared later that night. It did not, however, escape them that Jimmie was genuinely concerned about his friend's welfare.

Jimmie and Fred had overhauled Jimmie's engine in the number 0 car in preparation for an upcoming race. Jimmie was invited to participate in a race in Georgia, and Fred, Bill Blair and Bob Welborn tagged along that Saturday morning, just happy to be riding with their friends. They hitched the number 0 car onto the back bumper of Jimmie's streetcar, and took off. The others had quit teasing Jimmie about the number 0. His reply to them had been, "'Cause I like that number, that's why, and it ain't none of your damned business anyhow!"

Strong, heavy pieces of iron were welded into a cage on the front of number 0. They stuck out in front of the car approximately 12" and could be used as a battering ram should any driver refuse to let Jimmie pass. Metal tubing welded to the back took the place of a rear bumper, as a factory bumper would not last but a few laps in a wild and wooly race. Even the heavy tubing had numerous dents and scratches on it as it had become the target of a driver coming up from behind, anxious and determined to pass, even if it meant knocking the car blocking the path out of the way.

They arrived at the racetrack and Jimmie prepared to run it so as to see what his car could do. There was no speedometer on the car so it was difficult to tell how fast they actually went but they could tell if it was fast or not. Bill stood at the starting line and Bob paced off 50 yards ahead. Bob took his watch with the second hand out of his pocket and got ready to time him. He lovingly brushed the dust off as he watched the second hand clicking off the time. This watch was a gift from his daddy, who had gotten it from his daddy, so it was very special to him.

"Are you ready?" Fred took his handkerchief out of his pocket and held it in his left hand.

"Yeah, let 'er rip!"

The handkerchief dropped and Jimmie was off, tires squealing and the car swerving. He drove around the track once, gaining speed as he did. As he approached Fred, Fred dropped the handkerchief once more and Bob locked his eyes on the second hand of his watch.

"Three seconds!" he screamed as Jimmie roared by.

They were well pleased with the results of their test and decided it was a good engine. Other drivers began arriving and the group watched carefully as they each ran around the track to qualify. Unfortunately, about an hour before the race was to start, it began raining heavily. They sat in the cars, waiting patiently but morosely for the weather to clear, but it never did. Finally, after several hours, the race was called.

They were feeling disappointed as they headed back to North Carolina and home, but they were soon laughing and sharing "war stories" so their disappointment was forgotten. They had driven out of the rain and just outside the North Carolina border, they saw a sign on the side of the road advertising: Ice Cold Watermelons Ahead. It had stopped raining, would soon be dark and they were hungry.

"Hey, that sounds good," Bob observed. There was no air conditioning in the car and anything cold, especially a cold, sweet watermelon, sounded good.

Jimmie drove into the area in front of the small stand and stopped. They were a bit frustrated to see that the stand was unmanned. Not to be outdone, they decided to just leave $1.00 and take a watermelon anyway. Of course, they knew they weren't ice cold as they were just lying on a shelf under the open roofed stand but they were wet. And sweet.

Fred crawled out of the passenger seat, tucked a dollar under a watermelon at the edge of the pile and picked a large, green melon. He gave it the obligatory thump with his fingers as he had seen his mother do and they gathered around to eat it. The rind popped and juice squirted out as the small pocketknife belonging to Bob gnawed through the large fruit. Soon they had uneven chunks in hand and were enjoying the sweet, red meat. They laughed and dodged seeds as an impromptu seed-spitting contest and battle erupted. Their revelry was interrupted by a carload of teenagers passing their parked vehicles. A series of hoots, catcalls, whistles and obscenities greeted the picnickers.

Bob and Bill shouted back at the revelers, answering obscenity with obscenity, gesture with gesture. Jimmie became a little uneasy as the car initiated a three-point road turn and headed back to their site.

"Let's pack this up and get out of here," he commanded. "I don't like the looks of this. They could have guns."

The men scrambled back to their car as the teens passed them once again, hooting, cursing and challenging.

"Hey, old men, let's see what you got there! Let's see what kind of guts you got, Captain Zero!"

Jimmie entered the driver's seat and Bill got in on the passenger's side. The other two got in the back, Fred behind Bill and Bob behind Jimmie. They had all retrieved their watermelon except Jimmie. He had dropped his. He started the engine and pulled away as quickly as he could with the race car attached to the back.

It was beginning to get dark and Jimmie was feeling more and more uneasy about the way this situation was setting up. The carload of noisy teens wasn't about to back down and he didn't like being nervous. He kept the car in the middle of the road so that they couldn't pass. That only intensified their bullying and loud retorts.

"Pull over and let 'em come by me, Lew," Bill spoke.

"Hell, no, they might have guns. I ain't gonna let 'em pass. But I got an idea."

There was a dirt road cutting to the left of the paved road they were driving on and it was just ahead. There was a wide intersection where the dirt came into the pavement.

"Hold on!" Jimmie directed as he pulled onto the dirt.

He leaped out of the car, shouting, "Come on, give me a hand!"

They jumped out behind their friend, not knowing what he had in mind but trusting him just the same.

He jumped up beside the race car and began to unhook the tow bar.

"Let me at 'em! I'm gonna give 'em a run for their money."

Jimmie and his friends had worked very hard at building this new number 0 race car. It was equipped with a metal tubing roll bar and was surrounded by a metal cage in an effort to make it safer in the event of a rollover. The bumper on the front looked more like a battering ram than a bumper. The back bumper was constructed of metal tubing and was pockmarked with dents.

The drivers would approach the rear of an opponent, and if that opponent failed to move out of the way, the driver in back would gently kiss the bumper in front of him. Should the front driver fail to respond to the first kiss, another, more forceful bump would be given. If once again there was no attempt by the man in front to move over, a third, more determined bump was given. After the third warning, the driver attempting to pass would hit the bumper in front of him with the battering ram and the stubborn car refusing to move out of the way would slide sideways across the track in a spin out, careen wildly across the infield or sail through the air across a fence or ditch, and off the track.

Jimmie's tormentors had passed, their vision momentarily blinded by the dust from the dirt road that Jimmie pulled onto. They soon realized their error, and in their haste to turn around, ran off into a shallow ditch on the right. Five of them bailed out of the car to push while the driver steered and they soon were free of the ditch. The driver made the road turn, stopped, picked up his five companions and started back down the road. Jimmie sat behind the wheel of the race car, waiting for them to pass again. Bill climbed back into the passenger seat and Fred and Bob got in the back.

"Bring your watermelon!" Bill shouted.

They watched as the car made yet another road turn and as they came close to completing it, Jimmie accelerated and sped off ahead of them. He drove in the middle of the road, keeping them behind him.

"Let 'em pass!" Bill screamed.

"I told you no, they may have a gun!"

"Damn it, Lew, for once in your life, listen to me and don't argue! Let 'em pass!"

"Okay, but if I get killed, I'm gonna be severely pissed off at you, Blair."

"Just pull over and let 'em pass by me," Bill ordered. "Fred, get ready back there."

Soon the car loaded with screaming, jeering, cussing, hissing teenagers passed by on the right side of number 0. The driver leaned out his open window.

"Whadya say, old man? What you got in that old..."

Just as he was speaking, he was met in the face, full force, with the slab of watermelon Bill had been dining on earlier. At the same time, Fred let go of his slice and it hit on the support between the back and front windows, exploding into both the front and back seats.

As Bill and Fred drew back into the car, the vehicle beside them left the road, went down a large embankment and bounced across the open field toward the woods. Two beams of light would go up, then down, then up, then down. They laughed gleefully as Jimmie turned around, returned to the car to hook up the race car and continued their rudely interrupted journey toward home.

These men had deep love and respect for each other and did everything possible to take care of one another. They could be, however, vindictive of someone who treated them badly or did something to cause a problem.

Ralph McCoy was a driver from up North and would occasionally come down South to drive with the rebels. He was down one weekend and hitched a ride with Bill Blair to a race on a dirt track in Wilson, N. C. When they arrived, Ralph was offered a chance to drive a car belonging to a businessman from Wilson, and he, of course, jumped at the chance.

They were racing around the track and Ralph pulled up behind Blair. Bill kept him from passing and Ralph was becoming more and more frustrated. Finally, in desperation, Ralph tapped the back bumper of Bill's car and Bill skidded across the track into the fence. This was called spinning out a car and wasn't looked upon too kindly by the drivers; and was viewed as dirty pool, especially since Ralph had not made the traditional three warning taps. Bill recovered from the crash and managed to get back onto the track. He finished the race, but he hadn't forgotten what Ralph had done. Neither of the two won the race that day but when it was over, Ralph walked over to Bill's car and started to climb in.

"Where the hell you going?" asked Bill brusquely.

"I'm going back to High Point with you," Ralph answered, somewhat confused by the tone of his ride.

"No, you ain't neither. You ain't going with me."

"How come?" Ralph asked with surprise. It was assumed when he rode to Wilson with Bill that he would go back with him. That was a several hour trip and he had no other transportation.

"You S.O.B, you spun me out. You ain't gonna ride back to town with me."

"Then what am I supposed to do?" Ralph whined.

"I don't care what you do, but you ain't riding back with me," Bill stated emphatically. And with that he drove off, back toward High Point, Ralph standing in his rearview mirror on the side of that road in Wilson.

Bill France, who was a brilliant businessman, began to seriously develop his plan at organizing this rag-tag group of talent, guts and courage in 1947. In December 1947, he organized a meeting at the Streamline Hotel in Daytona. He had come to Daytona years earlier from Washington, D.C., and he operated a service station in Daytona. This allowed him to support his family as well as his racing passion. He observed how popular racing was becoming and how well known some of the drivers were becoming. Bill Blair, Jimmie Lewallen, Fred Harb, Lee Petty and Buck Mason were big draws at the racetrack.

People were also traveling across state lines to see races, especially if it was a well known driver. Bill France had a sense of fair play and decency, and wanted someway to ensure that drivers would not be cheated by promoters. He was also concerned by the frequent fighting and brawling and found it most distasteful. He felt that racing should be a family sport. Rules and fairness would help eliminate arguments and fights.

There must be a way, he thought, *that this can be better organized and made safer and more profitable.*

He spent many sleepless nights trying to decide how to help his friends and himself. Racing as it was being run had a bad reputation. Drivers were viewed by some as little more than outlaws, running illegal moonshine, outrunning the law, fighting and brawling on and off the racetrack. Yet they still appealed to the masses. There was something exciting to the public about these outlaws. It was similar to the Robin Hood fascination. There should be some way for him to harness and tame this raw energy and talent, turn it into a legitimate business. So he called his friends together at the Streamline Hotel.

"Fellas, I got an idea but I'm gonna need your help with it."

They all listened politely as he explained his plan.

"There's tons of money to be made out there with racing but we gotta get better organized. We need to quit fightin' and scrappin'. I'm asking you fellas to stick with me and make a small cash investment of a hundred dollars. You won't get no return on your investment right away, but if you stick with me, I promise I'll take care of you."

Most of the men were skeptical and uneasy about what he had in mind. The "small cash investment of a hundred dollars" didn't seem small to any of them, especially the married. They squirmed uncomfortably in their chairs. They worked full-time jobs, supported their families and kept their race cars together with what sometimes seemed like bailing wire and chewing gum. It didn't seem possible to any of them that they could come up with one hundred dollars.

"What we need," he continued, "is to get the promoters to put their money where their mouth is. We need to have them guarantee that we'll be paid when we win, and we can even get them to eventually pay a little to everybody that races, whether they win or not."

They all laughed aloud at that concept. Bill turned to Jimmie for support.

"Jimmie, you got a good head for figures. Whadya say? I could sure use your help in getting this thing off the ground."

"Naw," Jimmie responded. "It'll never fly, Bill. Besides, I wanta race. I ain't interested in starting no business like this. I gotta support my family, and I can't work at the Pontiac place, race and help you start a new business."

Jimmie Lewallen would later remark that was the biggest regret of his life.

France didn't give up on his dream. He had a few people who had confidence in his idea and he began to pursue his plan. Clay Earles, owner of the Martinsville Track in Virginia, partnered with him to get the idea off the ground. It was suggested by Red Vogt that the name of the organization be National Association of Stock Car Auto Racing.

"That sounds kinda complicated and why would we put *car* and *auto* both in it?" France questioned.

"'Cause the initials are NASCAR and that's easy for people to remember."

France's face lit up.

"So it is. Yeah, so it is. I like it!"

He sweated over developing rules and guidelines for the drivers. The first thing he wanted stopped was the fighting, especially on the tracks. It was dangerous as well as uncouth. He wasn't sure how to go about stopping the fighting so he decided that the best thing to do was hit them where it hurt the most – in the wallet. He would levy fines against drivers who broke rules.

Another issue that caused Bill France much distress was the problem with the women who followed the races. Since bibilical times, disreputable women have been camp followers, traveling with the armies of David and other warriors, entertaining the troops. There was no shortage of women admirers hanging around the racetracks during the early days. Most, however, were not there to drive – they were there to flirt and be close to the modern day gladiators and racetrack warriors who were so admired. The drivers called these women "baby dolls" and "fence huggers," so named because they hung over the fences, shouting and waving to the drivers. They would toss bits of paper containing their name and phone number to any willing driver. Many would also include their motel and room number. The willing drivers would burn up the night with the flames of alcohol and torrid women, living hard, drinking hard, loving hard and driving hard. They ran on adrenalin, booze, sex and guts.

At the track in Wilkesboro one practice day before a big race, the fence huggers were particularly aggressive and persistent.

"Hey, big boy, wanta have a good time?" one yelled. She tossed a piece of paper and it landed at the feet of Junior Johnson.

Junior stepped back, turned red, and began to stutter.

"Uh, uh, I gotta go. My wife's looking for me," and he made a hasty retreat.

The drivers standing nearby laughed heartily at their embarrassed friend.

Wives and girlfriends of errant drivers learned to behave in one of two ways over this issue. They either ignored the behavior, abhorring it but not willing to lose their man over it, or they walked away, unable to deal with the shame and degradation. Therefore, the divorce rate in the racing community was extremely high.

The first NASCAR-sanctioned race was held February 15, 1948, on the beach at Daytona. Red Byron from Atlanta won that maiden race. Six days later on February 21, 1948, the organization was incorporated. It was an immediate success with huge crowds showing up for every race. Drivers became instant celebrities and names like Fireball Roberts, Tim Ferguson, Jimmie Lewallen, Peewee Jones, Bill Blair, Fred Harb and Lee Petty became household names.

An accidental empire was rising from the dust, noise, sweat and blood of these early racers.

CHAPTER 3
Fightin' the Dust

It was an already hot, sultry July morning, typical of summer in the South, as the sun peeped cautiously over the trees around Tri-City Speedway. Bill Blair and his brothers had built this half-mile oval track just off Skeet Club Road in North High Point, N.C. They designed it with the one-mile track at Langhorne, Pa. in mind. The Langhorne dirt track was covered with recycled black motor oil, making it less dusty than most.

Elmer Kerns from High Point was employed to spread the oil on Tri-City and pack it into the surface in an attempt to keep down the choking dust. The first few races run at the speedway were motorcycles, and the drivers complained that they could get no traction on the oil slick surface.

The brothers went back to the drawing board with their design, had the oil scraped off the track and began to use calcium chloride mixed with water sprayed onto the surface. They would spray the track before a race and drive vehicles over it to pack it in. Sodium chloride is a coarse, salt-like substance that melts very slowly so it was somewhat successful in keeping down the dust for several hours. Many racing accidents were the result of the blinding dust, so the drivers welcomed this method of spraying.

Tri-City quickly became a favorite racing Mecca for drivers from both the immediate area and surrounding states. A high wooden fence surrounded the track in an effort to contain the cars as well as help ensure that spectators would purchase the quarter tickets for entry. However, trees surrounding the fence were almost always filled with people, usually young boys, watching the races. Bill made no big deal of these non-payers, as he understood the love of racing these children had. He too had shared their passion since he was very young himself.

The song of a cicada pierced the morning mist and early birds flitted about in search of the elusive worms, hiding deep in the ground, away from the merciless heat of the sun. Crickets and a bullfrog in a nearby creek sang their final notes as they, too, burrowed deep into the relative coolness of the earth to escape the burning orb of the Southern summer. This tranquil setting was soon shattered as automobiles began to roar into the racetrack area. Birds flew away in alarm as the cars scattered the mist and raised dusty clouds on the approach to the track.

The early morning was filled with laughter and eager conversation as the drivers greeted each other and prepared for the day's games. They had looked forward to this day all week, and the air was nearly electric with their excitement and enthusiasm.

It was 1948 and this was one of the early races sanctioned by the company newly formed by Bill France. Drivers from Georgia, South Carolina, Virginia and North Carolina were converging to spend the morning racing. Jimmie Lewallen, Bill Blair, Fred Harb, Junior Johnson, Peewee Jones, Tim Ferguson, Buck Mason, Glen Wood, Bill France, Lee Petty and Jim Paschal were all seasoned drivers, each with a number of wins under his belt and growing reputations as stars of the sport.

This day marked the maiden race for Robert Nooe of High Point. He had bought Johnny Tysinger's #6 car after Johnny had raced it at Daytona the year before. Baker's Tire Service had sponsored Johnny, and the name of the company was still painted on the side even though they did not sponsor Robert. Companies were beginning to see a source of advertising by giving these drivers some financial support in return for the company name being painted on the side of the car. Buck Mason, always a shrewd businessman, had seen the benefit of this several years earlier and had approached various garages and car dealerships for sponsorship. His peers, less extroverted and more conservative than he, had not subscribed to Buck's methods. They had no ambition to become rich or well known – they just wanted to race and to have fun with their fellow racers.

The men stood by the track with watches to time the drivers as one by one, they ran a lap around the track to qualify for their lineup position. There were no speedometers on the cars so they had no clue as to their actual speed. The watches, however, allowed them to see who was most likely the fastest, and they lined the cars up accordingly to start the race.

Soon the race was ready to begin, and Jim Paschal had been declared the pole starter. Jim was a great driver, energetic and forceful on the track. When crowded by another driver, he refused to relent and usually the other driver would back down. If not, one or both drivers would spin out across the track into the fence or the infield.

Jim loved to race and was respected, if not feared, by the other drivers. He did not, however, like the attention racing brought him from the fans and newspapers. He preferred to race, leave the track and go fishing. He abhorred the limelight and felt very uncomfortable discussing racing with anyone other than his fellow drivers. A very private person, he felt comfortable only when in their presence. They were his peers, his brothers and the ones with whom he identified.

Buck, on the other hand, loved the attention and was quite charming in talking to radio personalities or local news reporters about racing and his own role in it. Consequently, he was building a great reputation with the public as a race driver. Others had won more races and actually drove faster and better, but Buck was more aggressive in his public relations efforts. The public gravitated to the one who was willing to speak to them and that was Buck.

Robert placed tenth in the lineup and nervously waited for the flag starting the race to drop. He had done much street racing since he was just a kid, but this was his first race with real professional drivers. He would race with other cars, motorcycles, anyone who would accept his challenge on the streets. This, however, was the big time, the real thing, where the men were separated from the boys, the talkers from the doers.

The flag dropped and the cars sped from the starting line. The crowd erupted into cheers and screams, leaping to their feet in excitement. Robert moved up a couple of positions as he began to lose his uneasiness and get into the spirit of racing. He forgot about the crowds and the cars behind him, concentrating only on the cars ahead. He began to crowd Jimmie in his eagerness to pass. Jimmie moved up close to the fence, throwing dust as he steered to the edge of the track, in an effort to avoid Robert.

Robert went into a slide as he got dangerously close to Jimmie. He wasn't sure whether he made contact with Jimmie, or whether Jimmie had gently kissed his front bumper, but Robert was suddenly skidding the other way across the track, away from Jimmie. He jerked the steering wheel in an attempt to correct the skid, and his world turned upside down as the car flipped over. Somehow he came to a stop near the fence, still clinging to the steering wheel, suspended by the rope tied securely around his waist.

The tires were still turning, and he was confused and disoriented as his two younger brothers, Milford and Clayton, arrived on scene. They had been watching from a tree outside the fence, but managed to get to their brother before anyone else inside the track could reach him. They later stated they had no memory of how they got out of the tree and over the fence.

"Robert! Robert!" they both screamed. "Are you okay? Are you okay?"

He turned to look at them, unable to yet speak, but even upside down, he could see their relief as he met their eyes. The race was stopped, as was customary in early racing, and other drivers came to check on their friend.

"Are you okay, buddy?" Jimmie asked as he ran to Robert's window.

"Yeah, I think so, but you wrecked me."

"Naw, you did it to yourself, Rookie."

"You're crazy, Lew. You spun me out."

"You'll learn not to crowd somebody unless you can back it up, Nooe," Jim Paschal explained. "Let's get you outta there and make sure you didn't bust nothing important."

"Yeah, let's make sure you're in one piece. We know your mouth works okay," Jimmie joked, obviously relieved to find his friend unscathed.

The relief was evident as they all gathered around and gently removed the rookie from the overturned vehicle. The only visible injury was a small cut on the middle finger of Robert's right hand.

"How'd that one get cut, Nooe? Did you have it stuck up at me?" Jimmie inquired.

They all laughed, including Robert.

"Wonder how much damage I done to my car," he worried as he struggled to his feet.

It was resting on the roof, at the top of the windshield.

"Don't look like much damage. These Fords are built like tanks anyhow. Let's get it turned over and we'll take a look." Paschal leaned over, peering at where the roof of the car rested on the track.

Soon they had it back on all four wheels. Except for a small dent above the windshield and some deep scratches, the car showed little damage.

"You think you can drive her?" France asked.

"Yeah, if she'll start, I'll drive her."

The race began again. Buck had slipped by four cars after the wreck stopped the race, always ready to take advantage of any opportunity to get ahead.

From the beginning of his career, Buck had studied the other drivers and the conditions of various racetracks as the cars ran. He had a very analytical mind and quickly realized that the speeding, spinning, sliding cars tore up the dirt tracks very early in a race. Deep ruts and gouges created by aggressive drivers caused damage to cars. Things would break and bend and fall off, putting drivers out of the race. Various parts of the car and/or engine would fall off (including gas tanks), settling on the track, making the surface even more dangerous.

Buck drove defensively and carefully, calculating his moves, avoiding the ruts and debris and driving with cool determination instead of hotheaded passion. He would nudge someone to spin him out, only if the opportunity presented itself, but was sneaky with it, making it appear as an unintentional accident. He would fight with great ferocity if someone caused him to spin out, however. Therefore, Buck Mason won many races, not because he was necessarily the fastest but because he used different methods. It was his plan and ambition to be successful at racing and to become rich doing it. Woe be to anyone who got in his way as he climbed his ladder.

The family members or friends of the drivers stood on the sidelines, pads and pens in hand, anxiously counting the laps as each car passed. Their accuracy, or lack thereof, frequently determined the winner or loser of a race. They took their responsibilities very seriously, especially since prize money was now being awarded to winners.

As the first race ended after nearly an hour of hard running, Jim Paschal was given the winning flag. The crowd cheered and other drivers ran to congratulate him.

"Hey, hold on a minute! That ain't right. He didn't win! I did."

The crowd hushed and the drivers turned to see the familiar sight of Buck Mason objecting to the win.

"I finished a full lap ahead of Paschal! Here's my lap count," he continued.

The judges chosen to rule on the race huddled together, studying both Paschal's and Mason's lap scores. Mary Mason stood nervously behind her husband, biting her nails in anticipation.

Paschal stood nearby, his hands on his hips and a frown on his face. He was confident that he had won the race, but he had seen Buck's antics before. He knew his adversary was not above cheating to get a win and most of the time he received the backing of the judges. Bill France struggled diligently to do the right thing and make the correct calls in any challenge, but with the information available, France knew he sometimes probably made mistakes. However, everyone knew that he did the best he could.

In a few minutes, the announcement was made that Buck Mason was the winner of the race and Jim Paschal finished second. Buck beamed broadly and waved his arms to the cheering spectators. A few Paschal fans booed briefly. Paschal shook his head, muttered, "Damn," under his breath and walked away. The other drivers glared angrily at Buck, and Mary was obviously relieved. She ran to her husband to hug him, and he pushed her aside as he ran to pick up his purse of $25.

The mood at the Lewallen's home after the day's race was somewhat strained as the families gathered to share their customary meal together after a day at the tracks. The children were unaware of any issues or uneasiness and they played happily together. The women soon forgot the unpleasantness as they gathered around the baby girl, Rita Lewallen.

"I'm real sorry about the controversy at the track today, Jim," Mary offered quietly. She appeared self-conscious and uneasy.

Paschal made no comment, just nodded briefly and turned away.

Mary glanced at her friend Carrie, desperately seeking assurance. She was frequently embarrassed by her husband's aggressive tactics in challenging a win, but was helpless in doing anything about it. Carrie smiled kindly at her friend, patted her arm warmly and placed Rita in Mary's arms.

CHAPTER 4
Billy Blair, Women Drivers, Billy Biscoe and Charles Wickersham

Billy Blair sat quietly at his desk in his third grade classroom at Johnson Street School, anxiously watching the clock on the wall over the teacher's desk. Billy was a bright, intelligent, well-behaved child but had no interest in the assignment of copying spelling words over and over on his paper. His mind and heart were filled with memories of the previous day's races. He sat drawing race cars across the page in front of him while his classmates dutifully followed the assignment given by their teacher.

The teacher, Ms. Williams, was a stern lady who tolerated no nonsense in her class. Billy had learned that she probably had ESP, and possibly radar, and at least eight pairs of eyes, several of which were in the back of her head. He, therefore, learned to watch the clock very carefully, raising his eyes without moving his head. When she moved to look up, Billy would quickly divert his eyes back to the sheet of paper on his desk. Every few seconds, he would glance cautiously up at the clock. 8:25. He began to squirm nervously. It was the beginning of the school day on Monday morning, but he was behaving as if it was the end of the last day before summer vacation.

Another quick glance at the clock. Still 8:25. The teacher raised her head to check on her students, and he quickly dropped his eyes, avoiding her gaze. She perused the class to make certain everyone was on task. In a 1946 classroom, this was really not necessary as all the students of that era were generally obedient and well behaved. They knew if they weren't, they'd get what-for from their parents when they arrived home after school.

The clock's hands slowly, agonizingly crept along, finally resting at 8:28. Billy quietly pressed the end of his pencil onto the paper containing doodles of race cars and snapped the point off, careful not to allow a loud popping sound as the soft lead fell from the end of the pencil. He slowly slipped out of his seat and moved toward the pencil sharpener mounted in the window on the wide wooden sill. Ms. Williams glanced up, a frown on her face, and Billy raised his pencil silently in her direction to show her the reason for his leaving his seat. She nodded slightly, sighed softly and returned to her work, a frown still furrowing her brow.

Billy gazed out the window with eager anticipation, obviously looking for something. Soon he heard it and his heart leaped. A smile crept across his face and his eyes widened. Several of his classmates looked up, smiles across their faces as well.

Almost like clockwork, each Monday morning at 8:30 sharp, Jim Paschal would drive his race car by Johnson Street School on his way to Fred Harb's garage. Jim, Fred and Bill Blair, Billy's father, would spend Mondays working on their cars after racing them on the weekends.

Jim would slow down, lean out his open window and wave in the direction of Billy's classroom. If he saw Billy's smiling face at the window, he would gooch the accelerator, causing the deep voice of the powerful engine to reverberate across the schoolyard.

The other children in the classroom would squirm with excitement as the sound filled their ears, wanting desperately to run to the windows.

"Billy, sit down." Ms. Williams' voice was commanding.

"Yes, ma'am," he replied, hurriedly sharpening his pencil.

The teachers tired of hearing Billy talk about the weekend races, but his friends and classmates never did. The young race fan was the center of attention on the playground at recess and teachers would frequently break up their huddle to get the children back on the field to exercise and play.

The Blairs owned and operated a dairy farm on Lexington Avenue there in High Point. Drivers were traveling to races in South Carolina, Florida, Georgia, Bowman Gray in Winston Salem, Richmond and Pennsylvania almost weekly during the warm months. Lexington Avenue where the Blairs lived was also Highway 29/70 and drivers from up north would pass through North Carolina on their way to tracks in the south. Southern drivers would also pass by the Blairs on their way up North so it became tradition for them to stop and spend the night at the Blair dairy farm.

Billy was just a kid and was enchanted by these dashing drivers who spent so much time at his home. They would sleep in their cars and Billy would sit and watch and listen to them, his young brain absorbing their words and actions. The drivers would drink beer, or moonshine they were hauling, tell tales, play poker, tinker with their cars, and mainly talk racing. Billy would sit silently, worshiping these modern day swashbucklers, and storing all their words and activities into his memory.

In addition to being an intelligent young man, Billy had great capabilities and talents. His heart, however, was with racing. Even though his teachers wearied of hearing about racing, he never tired of talking about his first love.

"Come over here, Billy," Jim Paschal invited on one of these enchanted nights. The hood of Paschal's car was raised, and soon Billy was perched on the front fender, leaning over and peering into the soul of the race car.

"This here's a carburetor like none you've ever seen before. It's got four barrels and that means it'll make the engine run faster."

Billy watched in awe as other drivers gathered around, each eager to share their knowledge with this young man who adored them all.

Bill Sr. took Billy to the racetracks each weekend. In the summer after school was out, they would travel to the out-of-state tracks. Young Billy Blair continued to watch and listen, and would rest on the fenders of the cars, peering for hours into the engine area as drivers worked on the motors. It all began to make sense to him, and he was fascinated by the workings of these engines. He began to understand how all the lines and pistons and wires and spark plugs and gaskets worked together to propel a car around the track and over the finish line.

The drivers were impressed by Billy's interest and enthusiasm and began showing him how motors were put together and how they worked. They even allowed him to touch and work with and become familiar with the heart of a race car – the engine. His life's work was beginning to form. As an adult, Billy Blair would become a well respected and sought after builder of extraordinary racing engines. He would eventually build winning motors for such racing legends as Terry Labonte and Jim Paschal. The first race that Terry Labonte won at Darlington was with a Bill Blair motor. As Bill grew and matured, Jim Paschal would become his mentor, his hero and a great influence upon the young mechanical genius.

A different and exciting group of interested racers was becoming more visible on and around the red dirt tracks of the South. Women, who loved racing and driving and were dedicated to the sport, caught the attention of Bill France. He was always looking for a draw to get people to the racetracks, and he saw these women drivers as a way to draw spectators to events. He was quick to capitalize on their presence.

Predictably, some of the male drivers objected strongly to the presence of these powder puff drivers. Always a superstitious lot, many saw women as just another jinx and bad luck charm. Not to be deterred, Bill France basically told the men who objected to get over it or leave the track. Most decided to stay. So several women, including Evelyn Ferguson, Sara Christian and Louise Smith, actually became race drivers in the early days of the sport.

Biscoe Funeral Home in the Tampa Bay area of Florida operated the only ambulance service in the area during the early 1950s. The business was invited to attend all local sporting events with an ambulance in case of an accident.

Four-year-old Billy Biscoe was awakened early one morning by his father. It was his daddy's rotation to take the ambulance over to the race on the beach at Daytona. He loaded the child into the ambulance and took him along.

Bill France used the ambulances as safety equipment at the races and made certain there was always at least one from local funeral homes around the different racetracks. He cared about the welfare of drivers who had little safety equipment in their cars. He was learning with each race and each wreck what needed to be done to keep them as safe as possible, but he absolutely insisted on having ambulances on hand at the races.

Billy's daddy sat him on the hood of the large Cadillac ambulance.

"Sit here and watch these cars," he instructed his son.

Billy watched the cars slide around the corners of the makeshift beach track and drive out into the water. The beach was 500 feet wide and they would race down the sand, turn to go out onto the paved street, bounce back onto the beach, and run through the water. He was thrilled and curious about what he was seeing and pointed his tiny child finger in the direction of the cars in the water.

"Look at them cars, Daddy," he observed. "What're they doing?"

"They're cooling off their tires, son. The tires get hot running so fast so they run into the water to cool them down."

"Oh." His tiny eyes gleamed with excitement and pleasure as he watched the spectacle playing out in front of him. He never closed his mouth once during that race and frequently yelled his approval of what he was seeing. He nearly fell off the huge hood of the ambulance when Jim Paschal drove his car too far out into the water and was in up to the handle on his car door. He was greatly relieved when Jim managed to drive his car out of the deep water and return to the beach, dripping water, spinning tires and throwing sand. Young Billy's excitement was near delirium.

Evelyn Ferguson was racing that day on the beach and happened to be running against her brothers Bob, Floyd and Tim. She had qualified to start in the 11th position. It was a hard race that day and all three of her brothers left the beach before the end of the event, their cars plagued with mechanical problems. Evelyn stayed with it and finished fourth that day, but she never let her three brothers forget that she finished a race that none of them were able to finish.

"Yeah, yeah," she taunted them. "Who's the best driver now?"

They laughed in good nature at her teasing, obviously proud of their daredevil sister.

Billy Biscoe was afforded the opportunity of attending many sporting events throughout the South with his father and got very close to the action by sitting on the hood of the ambulance. He would also see football games, rodeos and races at the local short tracks. Best of all, it was free, but his very favorite events were the car races and the motorcycle races.

"Boy," his father would frequently scold him, "them's the most dangerous sports they is. If you don't quit being so excited about them, I'm gonna quit bringing you to the races. A body could get hurt real quick out there on them tracks, especially with the motorcycles. Got no protection around you at all and them cars ain't much better. A person's body takes the full brunt of a hit in them tanks."

As an ambulance driver and funeral director, the man had seen the consequences of what could happen to a human body in a high speed motorcycle or car wreck, and he didn't want that to happen to his son. His son, however, was not impressed by his father's warnings.

Sara Christian, another early woman race driver, loved the sport and in 1949, her second year of racing, she was high in the NASCAR point standings. She was racing in Atlanta that year in her new Oldsmobile, and one of the spectators was young Billy Biscoe, his eyes popping and heart racing.

During the race, she lost control and wrecked, flipping her car seven times, much to the horror of the spectators. Her husband Frank was watching from the sidelines and was running toward her car before it stopped rolling. Frank arrived at the scene ahead of the ambulance, frantically searching the inside of the car to see if she was okay.

"Sara? Sara?" he screamed.

She turned toward him, managing a weak smile. The car had landed on its wheels, and he stood anxiously at her window, holding her hands, until the ambulance arrived.

"Let me get you out, baby," he pleaded.

"No, leave me be, Frank. My back hurts. We'd better wait."

She was gently removed from the car by emergency personnel and transported to the hospital, Frank sitting anxiously beside her.

"Sara, I don't want you racing no more. It scares me to death. You gonna get killed if you don't stop." He was nearly in tears as he watched his wife who was in obvious agony.

Sara Christian had a broken back from that spectacular accident. It took nearly a year for her injuries to mend, and during the entire period of her convalescence, Frank begged and pleaded with her not to race anymore. After her recovery, she decided to race one more time at Reading, Pa., just to make certain that she could.

"I need to do this, Frank," she explained. "Just to be sure that I still can. I don't want to walk away without knowing. I don't want to carry a fear inside me for the rest or my life so I just need to know."

Frank was uneasy but reluctantly supported her. He tried to understand her concern, but he was terrified at the thought of her back on that red dirt track, tearing around it, hell-bent for leather. Sara did run that race in Reading that day. She finished second, but more importantly, she proved to herself that she could still do it. She had conquered her demons. Much to the relief of husband Frank, she never raced again.

Louise Smith was arguably the wildest and woolliest woman to ever run a racetrack. Her penchant for cussing and drinking and fighting rivaled the behavior of even Curtis Turner, racing's legendary bad boy. The male drivers were in awe of this crazy woman and didn't quite know what to make of her. She was unlike any female they had ever encountered, especially in the deep South where women are historically demure and soft. Louise Smith broke the mold of women drivers on the early racetracks.

Even after witnessing accidents such as the one suffered by Sara Christian, Billy Biscoe's passion was not deterred. He was hooked. He started to school and became what was colorfully referred to as an "ornery" child, failing a few grades and not doing well at all in school. He took an auto shop course when he was 14, which became a turning point in his life, and his parents were understandably worried about their son's disinterest in his studies. They discussed the problem and sat him down on the living room sofa after dinner one night.

"Son," his father began, "me and your mom want to make a proposition to you. You're doing real well in your auto shop course, and if you keep your grades at a C average or better on everything else for the rest of this year and pass your grade, we'll let you build a stockcar and race it on the tracks right around home."

Billy was ecstatic. That was all the incentive he needed and his grades immediately improved, he passed his grade, and busily started building his first race car at the age of 15.

He took his car down to the Sunshine Track near his home on a Friday night to run his first race. The man at the gate stopped him.

"What you doing here, sonny?" he asked.

"I came to race."

"You ain't old enough to race."

"Oh, yes, I am! You let me in there. I came to race!" Billy jumped out of his car and ran around the man, flailing his arms and kicking dirt, screaming and yelling to get inside that racetrack.

Finally, somewhat amused by the spectacle, the man allowed Billy into the racetrack. Young Billy sat tensely behind the wheel of his car, his knuckles white from gripping the steering wheel. As soon as the flag dropped, he shot across the starting line, hell bent for that finish line. He ran those three laps and later swore he doesn't even remember seeing another car. All he could see was that finish line. Billy Biscoe won that race. He was shocked when someone walked over to his car and handed him an envelope.

"What's this?" he asked.

"It's your winnings, boy. Ain't you never won before?" The people standing around laughed at Billy's innocence about the workings of a race.

"I ain't never raced before," he blushed. He reached out and took the envelope, smiling as he saw the $10 bill inside.

Another driver challenged the win, stating Billy couldn't possibly be old enough to race. The legal age was 18.

"There ain't no way this kid's 18," he accused.

Billy leaped out of his car and jumped on his accuser.

"You shut up!" he screamed. "I won this race fair and square, and it's mine!"

After peeling Billy off the challenger, a discussion was held among the track owner, several drivers and officials to make certain France's rules were followed at the races. It was decided that Billy Biscoe was indeed too young to race. They took his envelope away from him and escorted him out of the racetrack area. As he stood outside the fence beside his car, nearly in tears, the owner of the track approached him.

"Here, kid." He handed Billy a piece of paper. "This here's my IOU for $10. I want you to come back and race again. You're good. You can't win 'cause you ain't old enough, but I want you to race. You can get some experience out here running and the folks watching the race really liked your guts. You come back anytime and just tell 'em I told you it's okay."

Billy's early race car, which he built, was #33, but he had to change the number when he changed divisions. The #33 was being used in the Late Model Division by another driver, so his new number became #38. He used that number because he couldn't afford a sign painter, and it was relatively simple to change the 3 to an 8.

Charles Wickersham began drag racing in 1955 in Sarasota, Florida. He visited Daytona in 1959 and saw stock cars racing up and down the beach, and like so many others he, too, was hooked. He obtained his NASCAR license in 1959 and began stock car racing in 1960 at the Daytona 500. While still drag racing in 1958, he was named the Flying Rebel but that was soon shortened to Reb. Throughout his career until his retirement in 1966, he was known as Reb Wickersham.

Curtis Turner, always looking to make a fast buck, had the idea of building the Charlotte Motor Speedway in the 1950s. He convinced Bruton Smith to go in with him on the venture. The two were in way over their heads from the beginning with this venture.

The new Charlotte Motor Speedway in North Carolina built by Curtis Turner and Bruton Smith opened for the maiden race on June 19, 1960. The asphalt track was a new concept and even had pits for the drivers to pull into for service and repairs to their race cars. The new asphalt, however, was extremely soft and unstable, and as the cars practiced and qualified before race day on this mushy surface, the new track was torn up and nearly destroyed.

Curtis was also driving that day, attempting to qualify for the race.

"Damn, Bruton, what the hell we gonna do about all this crap flying around?" Curtis was distraught as he approached his partner.

"I don't know." Bruton shook his head. "This is awful. I don't know what we're gonna do."

Large chunks of asphalt were flying and drivers were pulling off the track, gathering together in groups, trying to decide what to do.

"Maybe you can put wire or screen or something in front of the radiators," Bruton suggested. He was obviously worried and upset over this turn of events.

Drivers took his suggestion and were soon going all over Charlotte to hardware stores, even farm supply stores, trying to find something, anything to protect their engines from flying asphalt and tar. Pieces of metal or wire mesh, anything that they thought might help protect their expensive engines were placed under the hoods and in front of radiators in an attempt to add some precious protection. Ingenious drivers constructed steel boxes covered with chicken wire and installed them on the front of the cars to help keep asphalt out of the motors.

The day of the race proved to be even more trying and difficult. The cars driving around the new track pressed grooves 6" to 8" deep, creating tremendous ruts and bumps. It was much like racing over a track covered with huge speed bumps. Cars and drivers were bouncing everywhere in an attempt to complete the first World 600 race.

After just a few laps, drivers were forced to pull into their pits, a new experience for them all, and try to remove hunks of tar and asphalt from their hoods, bumpers, screen protectors and windshields. Buren Skeen lost a wheel around a curve, and it flew over the fence, bouncing down the high bank into the field below, barely missing a number of cars parked there.

People who were parked in the area, unable to afford a ticket for admission, watched in disbelief as the tire bounced over and over, down the bank, across a field and finally into a deep gully. This only intensified their wishes to be inside the track where the action was.

"This is a damn mess," Reb Wickersham declared. "I ain't never seen nothing like it. If this track don't tear up my car and me as well, it'll be a miracle."

The event took six or seven grueling hours to complete and Joe Lee Johnson won the first ever World 600 race at the Charlotte Motor Speedway.

"That was a helluva ride!" Joe Lee commented as he stood in Victory Lane. He reached over and picked out large chunks of asphalt from the wire cage gracing the front of his car.

Other drivers stood around pulling and picking asphalt off their cars, uniforms, arms and faces. The track was shut down afterward for repairs to the pavement, and it was questionable as to whether it would ever re-open. Many of the cars were destroyed by the harsh conditions and drivers were physically and mentally exhausted. It was a very difficult day for everyone. Even the spectators were covered with bits of asphalt and tar, and removing the muck took skin off faces and arms.

"Well, I reckon all we need are the feathers," one genial spectator commented as he left the stadium. "We're all pretty well coated with tar!" The surrounding crowd laughed good-naturedly with him.

The drivers and new owners of this nightmare were much more distressed than the fans. Drivers normally lost 15 to 20 pounds during a race, and the first World 600 took off even more weight than that. Bruises and cuts and aching muscles, sprained backs, necks and bloody hands only added to the miseries of the day.

Charlotte Motor Speedway was off to a rocky start and things would get much worse before they got better. After several years, Smith and Turner declared bankruptcy but Smith was able to get back into it later with other investors. It went on to become one of the sport's premier and most popular tracks but the history of those early days would be legendary in the stories and memories of early drivers.

Reb was a close friend to fellow driver Jimmy Pardue. In 1964, Jimmy was testing tires at the Charlotte track. There was no race on this day, but tire manufacturers paid drivers to test their tires to see what would work best during these high speed and grueling races. As Pardue tore around the track, wiggling the steering wheel in an attempt to place stress on the tires, one of the front tires suddenly blew out. Jimmy was driving in excess of 100 MPH when it blew and the force turned him end over end, then into multiple rollovers.

When the car finally came to a standstill there was little left of it. The engine and roof, hood, fenders, trunk, and many indistinguishable pieces of carnage lay strewn for several hundred yards.

It took several minutes to locate Jimmy's body, as it was impossible to tell which way was up on the vehicle. He was finally located underneath what was left of the frame, his mangled body barely recognizable.

Jimmy was killed instantly, much to the sorrow of Reb and many others.

"We lost many drivers in those days," Reb explained quietly years later. "We were learning about the sport and about safety only through the deaths and injuries of the drivers. It was a hard thing to be driving in those days. But we loved it."

RED DIRT TRACKS

The speedway at Darlington, South Carolina was built by Bill France and became the granddaddy of stockcar racing. Reb was driving in the Southern 500 in Darlington on September 13, 1965, with many of the veteran drivers. Buren Skeen was running in front of Reb. Another car came very close to Buren, and it was later determined that Buren probably panicked as this speeding vehicle approached him. Buren hit his brakes and skidded sideways down the track. Reb saw the car skidding and knew that he wasn't going to be able to stop his own speeding vehicle. Reb stood up on the brakes in an attempt to avoid hitting Buren's car. In spite of all the valiant efforts he could muster, Reb struck Buren's car broadside, at the driver's door.

These early race cars were built of heavy steel and were much like tanks. A collision would bend them but they did not often disintegrate as modern day vehicles do, so the driver would take the full brunt of a hit. Current race cars will fall apart, taking the force of a hit rather than transferring it to a driver.

Reb sat there, stunned and in shock, and then everything went black. Rescue workers arrived quickly on the scene.

"Skeen's moving so we need to get Reb out first," one rescuer shouted. "Reb's car is on fire! Move, move, move!"

Reb was quickly removed from the burning car and placed on a stretcher.

"Get him on to the ambulance. We'll check on Buren."

The rescuers ran to Buren's car. One of the men looked at the other. "This don't look good. I thought he was moving, but it looks like his guts is hanging out of his mouth."

When Buren Skeen was gingerly removed, it was discovered that the force of the impact had dislodged his internal organs, actually choking him to death. That was a common and heart wrenching occurrence during the early days of racing.

Reb was unconscious for 13 hours. When he awoke, he looked around to get his bearings.

"How's Buren Skeen?" he asked a nurse standing nearby.

She made no comment but ran outside to summon the doctor.

"How's Buren Skeen, doc?" Reb asked as soon as the doctor appeared.

"I don't have a patient by that name. You've been through a bad accident so I just need you to rest."

"How long have I been out?"

"Awhile. There's a couple of men who have been waiting out here for quite a while to see you. Do you feel like visitors?"

"Yeah, let 'em in. Maybe they can tell me something. You sure as hell ain't gonna tell me nothing."

Jim Paschal and Jimmie Lewallen came into his room, still wearing their dirty and sweaty racing clothes.

"How you feelin', Reb," Jimmie asked.

"Kinda numb right now but nothing don't hurt too bad, I reckon. How's Buren?"

Jimmie glanced uneasily at Jim, then dropped his eyes.

"Damn," Reb murmured. "I'm real sorry. I just couldn't miss him."

"You did all you could, Reb," Paschal assured him.

Reb was knocked out of racing by his injuries for a long period of time. The death of Buren Skeen weighed heavily on him as well, and he began to drift away from stockcar racing. He knew there was no way that he could have avoided hitting the young driver, but the guilt was painful just the same. He couldn't erase the memory of Buren's face, filled with surprise and shock, as Reb sped uncontrollably toward him. While still convalescing from that wreck, Reb started speedboat racing and continued that until 1974. He quit stockcar racing completely in 1966, the face of Buren Skeen still burned into his memory.

The early drivers owned their own cars and had to do all of the work on them without much help from anyone other than friends or family. They would be running 180 to 185 MPH without the safety equipment of today. Their injuries and deaths helped develop today's safety equipment such as the window net and various safety belts and harnesses. The surviving drivers carry the scars, aches and pains, even today, of those early experiences. They also carry the emotional scars of losing friends and being involved in fatal accidents on the racetrack. Those experiences have taken a toll on the psyche and hearts of these sensitive men. Logically, they know there was no way to have avoided an accident that took a life but emotionally, the guilt pervades. The old questions, "what if," or "if only" haunt them, even today.

CHAPTER 5
Birth of the Pit Crew

The fightin' forties were over, most of the drivers were married and had young families, and Bill France was organizing the group to become more and more efficient and less rowdy with every passing racing season. The sport was becoming wildly popular and the drivers were becoming household names.

Wade Sykes stood on the sidelines at the Tri-City track, watching the cars speed around, stirring up clouds of red dust. The calcium chloride sprayed on earlier was quickly evaporating from the effects of the hot July sun as well as the heat generated by the tires. Wade had long had a burning desire to race, but knew there was no way he could afford the sport. He glanced fondly down at Mike, and smiled gently as he placed his hand on his son's head. The child looked up and smiled warmly at the father he adored. Mike moved closer, leaning against the comfort of his dad's tall leg.

Wade was a sensitive and responsible man who placed caring for his family number one on his list of priorities. However, he loved these drivers like brothers and did everything he could to help them. A carpenter by trade, he nonetheless stood by on the sidelines to help in anyway possible. He would roll tires to the cars, help change them, put gas in the tanks, give water to the drivers, whatever needed to be done. He became the very first unofficial pit crew in racing. There was no monetary pay for his work, and he would not have accepted any had it been offered. He was just glad to be at the races with his friends, sharing in the excitement. Jimmie Lewallen thought having a pit crew was a great idea. He appreciated all the help he got from Wade, but knew one man couldn't be everywhere.

It was a Saturday night after a race in Washington, D.C. Jimmie had won a $1000 purse, which was a huge amount of money at that time. It had been a 100 mile race and extremely hard on the drivers. Most of them had bloody hands from fighting the steering wheel, and all were totally exhausted. As was his custom after a win, Jimmie took all the drivers and their families out to dinner at a local restaurant near the track. A family of four could eat for $15 and so he fed ten families for about $150.

They were sitting around after the meal, laughing, talking, sharing stories about their racing, and just enjoying each other's company in general.

"Wade," Jimmie turned to his friend, "I want you to know how much we all appreciate what you do for us. You're a good friend and I like your style. What you do is a good idea, but I know you can't be everywhere at one time."

He turned to Carrie's brother-in-law Charlie Skeen and her brother Frank James, who had driven up from North Carolina to watch the race.

"Fellas, I want you two to be my pit crew in next week's race at Rockingham. Would you like to do that? I'll give you each a couple dollars, I reckon."

"Yeah, yeah, we'd love to!" they quickly agreed. They were obviously thrilled to be even a small part of the action.

At the Rockingham track the next weekend, Charlie and Frank rushed to Jimmie's car each time he pulled into the pit. After they filled his tank with gas at one such stop, he leaned out to shout instructions for his next stop.

"Now, boys, when I come in after the next lap, one of you have the jack and tire tool ready and the other have the tire. As soon as I pull in, run just as hard as you can. I'm gonna replace that left front tire. It's looking a little worn."

It was hard for them to contain their excitement as they waited for Jimmie to make another lap. Charlie clutched the tools tightly in his sweating hands, and Frank stood, holding the tire, poised to run. As Jimmie pulled in for his tire change, they took off running toward him as fast as they could. Jimmie watched from inside his car in total disbelief as the two men crashed headlong into each other and fell to the ground, both knocked out cold.

"Damn!" Jimmie muttered as he crawled out the window. "Guess I'll change my own damn tire!"

He gathered up the tools and tire, scattered around the unconscious men, and changed the tire as quickly as he could. When he pulled back onto the track, Charlie and Frank were beginning to stir a little.

He ran a few more laps and pulled into his pit area. He jumped out of his window and ran to the cooler of water he brought to each race. As he started to dip some out to drink, he noticed it was red and muddy looking.

"What the hell happened to my water?" he questioned his pit crew.

"Oh, I had all that red dust on me so I washed off a bit," Charlie explained.

"You crazy fool, that there's my drinking water!"

Jimmie chased him around the car, but Charlie managed to escape. Jimmie was still sputtering mad as the crawled back into his car to resume the race, but he laughed about their antics later.

The group gathered in the Lewallen's yard the following week, frying chicken and sharing good times. Jimmie told the story of his pit crew's actions the week before. Charlie and Frank hung their head in embarrassment but laughed along with the others.

"Yeah, it was funny when I pulled in to get my tire changed and they ran smack into each other. There was my pit crew, laid out cold on the ground. But weren't so funny at the time when Charlie trashed my drinking water. I got mighty thirsty in that race." He chuckled as he shook his head in disbelief and amazement.

Tiny Lund's small brown and white terrier was running around the yard, playing with the kids. Rita Lewallen, now a toddler, was enchanted by the little animal. She let out a sudden scream and waddled toward the street, only to be intercepted by her mother. The tires of a car screeched and the little dog yelped as a thump silenced the group. Tiny rushed into the street and gently picked up the injured pet.

"I'm sorry, mister, I couldn't get stopped." The driver was greatly distressed. "Is he okay?"

"I don't know," Tiny murmured worriedly. Rita was crying hysterically and the other children were grouped around in a worried knot.

"Guess you'll have to put him down, Tiny," Jimmie observed sadly.

"Naw, I ain't gonna do that 'less'n I hafta. I'll take him over to the vet's house. He may be able to help him out."

The children were relieved that Tiny was going to take the little dog for treatment instead of euthanasia, and stood anxiously by as he gently loaded him into the car for transport. They stood bunched together, watching as he drove down the street. Some were crying openly and others, like Tommy Mason, were trying to choke it back bravely. The boys didn't want anybody seeing them cry.

The mood was decidedly quieter until about an hour later when Tiny returned, carrying Bobo in his arms. The kids swarmed around him, peering anxiously at Bobo.

"The vet says he's just bruised a little and has a little cut on his front paw. He'll be sore for a spell but he should be okay. The next couple of days will determine whether he makes it or not," Tiny explained to the circle of anxious young faces surrounding him. They all wanted to hold him but Tiny laid him down gently on some towels Carrie had brought into the yard.

"Just leave him be, youngins," she admonished. "He don't feel like being bothered right now."

They sat quietly on the ground, surrounding him, speaking soothing words and giving gentle strokes to their little friend.

One of the first orders of business the next week at the racetrack in Wilkesboro was to check with Tiny about little Bobo's condition.

"He's doing good," he explained to the anxious children. Most of the adults were likewise relieved to hear the good news.

The wives counted the laps during the race in Wilkesboro, carefully seeking out the numbers on their husband's cars. This was serious and they wanted to do a good job. They sat on the front row of the grandstand with the children placed in a safe area further back, out of the way and instructed not to bother the mothers during the race. They knew the importance of these instructions, and being good kids, they listened to their mothers.

Jimmie won the race and the crowd was screaming and shouting their approval. He drove back to the stadium area, jumped out of the window and looked up at Carrie.

"Hand me Rita!" he smiled.

The child was passed from her mother to others, lifted over the short wall in front of the bleachers and placed in her daddy's waiting arms for a hug and a big kiss.

"Here, sweetheart, stand on the running board," he instructed his daughter.

Rita was placed on the running board beside the driver's door and Jimmie reached his strong arm out of the window. He wrapped it snuggly around her, the victory flag was placed in her tiny hands and he drove out onto the track. He made a victory lap with his four-year-old daughter smiling and waving the flag to the crowd. She was dressed in a white dress of lacy organza, white socks with lace around the top and tiny black patent slippers. Her blond curls lay on her shoulders and a pink bow held her hair off her face.

The crowd went wild as the child waved eagerly and proudly to them. They came to their feet, smiling, waving and screaming, "Little Lew, Little Lew!"

Jimmie pulled back into his pit area and Carrie tenderly removed Rita from the running board. As Jimmie crawled out of his vehicle to accept the winning purse, a voice called across the area.

"Hey, wait a minute, wait a minute there! That ain't right. Lew didn't win that race, I did."

They turned to see the familiar face of Buck Mason approaching the group, Mary tagging close behind.

"I finished a full lap ahead of Lew."

"No, you didn't, Buck," Tiny Lund objected. "You lost a whole lap when you changed your tire."

"I didn't change no damn tire! You're crazy."

The officials looked at the drivers, together and ready for a fight. Jimmie leaned back against his car, his legs crossed and his arms folded over his chest, just silently watching Buck.

Several of the drivers argued with Buck, swearing to the officials that Buck had stopped to change a tire and lost a full lap.

"All of y'all're crazy. I didn't change no damn tire. You're just trying to lie so Lew'll win."

"No, Buck, that's not right. You did change a tire." His wife Mary moved up beside him, the score sheet in her hand. She was holding it up and pointing to it.

"See? Right here. You did stop to change a tire," she explained.

Suddenly, without warning, Buck backhanded his wife across her face. Caught off guard, she tumbled over the hood of his car and onto the ground in front of the bumper. A gasp went up from everyone in the vicinity, and Carrie clamped her hand over her mouth to stifle a scream. She immediately rushed to her friend's aid. Tommy appeared from nowhere, stood in front of his father, his fists clenched by his side.

"If you ever do that again, there's gonna be big trouble," he muttered through clenched teeth. He glared angrily into his father's eyes before turning to assist his mother.

Jimmie was still leaning against his car, his eyes hard and cold as he stared at Buck.

"What the hell you looking at?" Buck smirked.

"I ever see you do that again, I'll kick your ass," Jimmie promised.

"You ain't gonna kick nobody's ass, and it ain't none of your business anyhow."

Jimmie uncrossed his legs, pushed himself off the side of his car and strode over to Buck. Jimmie stood right in Buck's face, pointed his open right hand almost in Buck's eye and repeated, "I ever see you do that again, I'll kick your ass."

Jimmie never raised his voice, but there was blood in his eye. Buck stared back at him for a brief period, then snorted and turned away. He kicked at a dirt clod as he walked away. Jimmie was confirmed to be the winner of the race and the behavior of Buck Mason on that day pretty much ended the friendship between the Masons and the Lewallens. Buck was declared second in the race but none of the drivers cared. As far as they were concerned, he was a loser, no matter what position he finished a race.

The 1952 racing season ended with Jimmie Lewallen and Bill Blair doing very well on the tracks. Peewee Jones was also burning the track up at Bowman Gray Stadium in Winston Salem. The following year, Little Lew was presented a tiny, white jacket with a 0 on the back and her nickname embroidered across the shoulders, along with a tiny helmet displaying her name. She wore them proudly to each race she could attend, and when her father won, she was placed on his running board for the victory lap. She quickly became the sweetheart of the racing circuit, and would carry in her heart and mind the forever memory of her victory laps with her beloved daddy.

"Little Lew! Little Lew!" the adoring crowd screamed, every fan on their feet.

The family was watching a race in New Jersey near the end of the racing season in the mid '50s. Rita was playing happily in a sandbox situated in the infield of the oval dirt track. Her mother was standing nearby, keeping a watchful eye on Little Lew, making certain she was safe as well as didn't mess up her uniform should Jimmie win the race. Young Richard Petty, now a teenager, sat on the edge of the sandbox, his feet resting in the sand. He enjoyed watching Rita play and would even help her fill her sand bucket if she asked for his help.

Suddenly, there were tires screeching and Richard looked up to see an out-of-control car careening toward the sandbox. He quickly grabbed Rita under her arms and ran from the area, carrying her and himself to safety. Carrie screamed and rushed to them as the car came to a stop just short of hitting the sandbox. She grabbed her daughter, holding her close as the other families hurried to her side to make certain everyone was okay.

"Thank you, Richard," Carrie gasped, her eyes filled with tears and gratitude to this young hero who had acted so quickly. "I ain't never gonna forget this and neither is Rita. We'll be forever indebted to you."

Richard smiled slightly, hanging his head in embarrassment.

"Ah, it wasn't nothing, Mrs. Lewallen. Anybody'd done it."

"Well, I'm just so glad you were there and acted as quickly as you did," she continued. "You sure got good reflexes."

Nobody would be surprised that this youthful hero, Richard Petty, would eventually become the King of Racing, and an honored and respected gentleman nationwide.

At the end of the racing season the year Rita was five years old, life settled into a routine as the family quit traveling the racing circuit for the season. Local racing friends, such as the Harbs and Blairs, as well as the Pettys, would still gather from time to time to visit and share a meal.

That winter, there was a particularly heavy snow. Jimmie would take a job anywhere he could find one after the racing season so as to support his family during the winter. That year he was driving a large delivery truck for Cheerwine. The Cheerwine is a popular soft drink available only in North and South Carolina, as well as Virginia. It is bright red in color and tastes very much like cherries. In the 1950s, there were no aluminum drink cans and all soft drinks were bottled in glass.

In preparation of making a delivery on Saturday morning, Jimmie loaded the truck in Winston Salem and drove it back home to Archdale on Friday afternoon. He parked it in the driveway, and the family went to bed early that night. It was extremely cold with the temperatures dropping into the teens during the night so Jimmie knew the streets would be particularly treacherous the next morning as the snow froze into solid ice.

Rita crawled out of her warm bed after daylight the next morning and ran into the living room to peep out the window at the large truck parked in their driveway. As she peeped out the curtains, she let out a scream.

"Daddy, Daddy, come quick! There's blood all over the driveway!"

Jimmie and Carrie were in the kitchen drinking coffee and ran into the living room to see what had happened. Jimmie let out a moan as he peeped out at the carnage frozen all over the driveway. He knew immediately what had happened. He quickly dressed and ran outside, pulling up the rolling metal cover that covered the sides of the delivery truck. Too late, he realized his error. Hundreds and hundreds of broken Cheerwine bottles fell crashing onto the driveway, their contents lying ominously on the ground surrounding the truck.

Pete from across the street came running outside.

"What happened?" he shouted across the street. "Did you hit a deer? Looks like it mighta been a whole herd of 'em."

"Naw," Jimmie replied, "the bottles froze and busted, and all the Cheerwine is laying out here on the ground. And like a fool, I lifted this cover and now I got glass all over the ground."

"You got a mess all right, neighbor, that's for sure. I'll bring some 55-gallon drums over here and help you shovel up the glass. Then we can load it on my pickup and take it down to the dump."

"I appreciate that, Pete, but if you just bring the drums over, I'll take care of shoveling all this up. I sure ain't gonna lift the cover on the other side of the truck 'cause I'm sure they're all broke on that side too. I made this mess and I'll clean it up."

For several hours, Jimmie labored in the cold and ice, shoveling up broken bottles and putting them in drums, all the while trying to keep from sliding down in the frozen red syrup. Cars would drive by slowly, occupants staring and trying to figure out what had happened.

One car stopped and a man rolled down his window.

"You hurt?" he questioned.

"Naw, I'm okay, thanks." Jimmie didn't even look up from his shoveling.

Not certain what to do, the man sat there for a few minutes and finally drove slowly off. He wanted to ask what happened but was afraid to.

I reckon his family's okay. Surely that ain't blood out there, he worried as he drove away.

After several hours of shoveling, Pete and a few more neighbors came over and they all picked up the heavy drums, setting them in the back of Pete's truck. Jimmie crawled into the passenger seat with him and they took the broken mess to the dump.

Jimmie drove the large Cheerwine delivery truck back to Winston Salem, got another load of Cheerwines, drove back to High Point, and delivered his load. The empty truck was returned to Winston, Jimmie picked up his personal car and got home just before dark, the driveway still stained blood red, and cars still driving by slowly, trying to figure out what happened at that home.

The next day after church, Jimmie decided to take his family for a ride in the snow and get away from the red stain and curious stares of people driving by their home. Jimmie loved to drive in the snow and he usually took Carrie and Rita with him, unless the roads were slick with ice. Carrie bundled up Rita, as there was no heater in the car, and slipped her into the back seat, cautioning her to sit still. There were no seat belts in the 1940s and 1950s, so Rita always sat quietly in the back seat, her short legs stuck out in front of her.

They rode up Main Street in High Point, one of the few paved streets in the city. Rita could see the trees and tops of buildings as they passed and could tell how deep the snow was. The trees were weighed down with the heavy, white pillows and windowsills of buildings had several inches of the powder piled up.

They drove to Winston Salem before Jimmie turned around and headed back to High Point toward home. Jimmie stopped the car at the traffic signal at Lexington Avenue and N. Main Street. The old Leonard Drug Store was on the corner and it was a rather steep hill at that intersection. They sat there, waiting for the light to change.

Jimmie was wearing an overcoat and a fedora hat. Rita watched her daddy as they sat there, thinking that he looked so much like the actor Broderick Crawford who played on the TV show *Highway Patrol*. A car pulled up behind their car, and the guy bumped them in the rear bumper.

Jimmie looked up into the rearview mirror and said, "That's one."

"Jimmie, don't," Carrie implored.

"Hush," he stated.

Rita sat silently in the back seat, but she sensed something was about to happen. The car behind them rolled backward once more, the man inched forward, attempting to get some traction, and he hit the Lewallen vehicle again.

Jimmie said, "That's two."

"Jimmie, don't do nothing."

"I said hush."

Rita was still sitting quietly in the backseat but she was sitting up very straight now, bracing for what would happen next. The light remained red. The man in the back pulled up and hit Jimmie's rear bumper a third time. Jimmie pulled up the emergency brake, turned the motor off and exited the car.

"Jimmie, please don't do nothing," Carrie implored, but her pleas fell on deaf ears.

It was slick on the street and Jimmie was having difficulty walking. He held onto the side of the car until he got to the front of the car behind them. He held on, working his way to the driver's side. The man lowered his window, and Jimmie leaned down to say something to him. By then, Rita had turned around, was sitting on her knees, watching the drama unfold behind her. Just as Jimmie started to say something, the man made a remark, and Jimmie's massive fist shot forward, landing in the center of the man's face. Jimmie made no response to whatever comment was said, but simply turned and made his way back to his car, holding onto the side so as not to slip down. He crawled back into the car.

Rita was laying in the back seat, laughing.

"Oh, Jimmie," Carrie sighed, "what have you done?"

He didn't answer, started the car and drove through the intersection, continuing home.

Oldtime race car takes victory lap

Jimmie Lewallen's car loses tire during race

Knocking down fences, 1947

Mike Sykes in Jimmie Lewallen's number 0 car

Going through fences, circa 1940s

"The King" Richard Petty with Gail Gurley

Ned Jarrett and Gail Gurley

At the racetrack, circa 1940s

Dust on the racetrack, circa 1940s

Jim Paschal and Jimmie Lewallen trading cards.

CHAPTER 6
Peewee Jones and the Myers Brothers

Saturday night wouldn't be Saturday night in Winston Salem without a race at the Bowman Gray Stadium. Peewee Jones was preparing to race, as he normally did on a Saturday. Peewee was, and is, the undisputed consecutive champion at Bowman Gray. He was champion six times and the only driver ever who was named five years consecutively. He was reigning champ from 1956 through 1960, and again in 1967.

On this particular day, Billy Myers had the pole position, Peewee was on the outside and Glenn Weddle was behind Peewee. Johnny Bruner, the flag man, always had a large cigar clamped between his teeth. Peewee had noticed that as Bruner was ready to throw the flag to start the race, he'd bite down on his cigar and it would move up from the bite. Peewee knew when the cigar moved up, the flag was coming down. Peewee held a crumpled paper drink cup in his hand, waiting for that cigar to go up and intent on distracting Billy just as the flag was ready to drop. He watched carefully and waited, anticipating the movement of that cigar.

They drove slowly around the track, behind the pace car,

staying in position and watching for the starting flag to drop. Peewee, however, had his eye not on the flag but on Bruner's cigar. Bruner bit down on that cigar, it rose up in his mouth, and Peewee cut loose with that crumpled cup. It flew across Billy Myers' hood, momentarily distracting him as he leaned over; glaring in the direction it took, trying to figure out what just flew by.

That was all the advantage Peewee needed, and as the flag dropped, he and Glenn both beat Billy into the first turn. They laughed to themselves all the way around the first lap. Tim Ferguson from Atlanta won that day, but Glenn and Peewee were acting as if they had won. They approached Billy after the race, laughing and slapping each other on the back.

"What's so funny?" Billy demanded.

"What was that flying across your hood, Myers?" Glenn asked, winking at Peewee as he did.

"What the hell you fellas know about that? Did you have a hand in something?" Billy was always suspicious of his two friends. They were frequently pulling some sort of stunt on each other and other drivers.

"Scared of a little old paper cup?" Peewee grinned.

"Damn, Jones, I oughta bust your ass!" Billy was angry but he was soon laughing along with his friends.

The following week at the track in Greensboro, Ted Swaim became the target of Peewee and Billy Myers. Bill France had succeeded in curbing some of the fighting so the drivers turned their attention and energy in the direction of tormenting each other and playing jokes. Peewee and Billy usually made a point, as much as possible, to be on either side of Ted. On this particular day, Peewee sat on Ted's left. They drove around the track behind the pace car, holding their positions. Generally when the flag dropped, Ted shot out in front of both Peewee and Billy.

Today as they approached the flag, Peewee took aim and flipped his cigarette out the passenger window and over Ted's windshield. Ted looked in stunned surprise, trying to see what flew by. That brief delay in Ted's reaction was all his two friends needed, and they roared off ahead of him. He soon caught up with and passed them both, however.

Six laps around, Billy pulled into his pit for a tire change. Ted saw him pull in and took the opportunity to likewise get a tire change. As his crew jacked his car up, Billy spun out of his pit and back onto the track. Ted looked in open surprise as he saw Billy's car pull out.

"How'd he get that tire changed so damn quick?" he yelled at his crew. As soon as he said it, he realized that he'd been had. Myers wasn't changing a tire. He was just messing with Ted.

Myers and Jones would frequently use the ploy of pulling in for a false pit stop, drawing other drivers in, and then they would return to the racetrack to get ahead. They enjoyed worrying their friends on the track nearly as much as they enjoyed racing. Billy would worry his racing brother Bobby the same way, every chance he got when they were on the same racetrack, but Bobby soon got wise to his practical-joking brother. The two frequently raced together and kept an eye on each other's positions. Bobby Myers learned early on not to make a pit stop just because his brother Billy or Peewee Jones did.

On September 2, 1957, the Myers brothers were scheduled to race against each other at the Southern 500 in Darlington, S.C. Bobby was driving a brand new 1957 Oldsmobile for Petty Enterprises. The brothers stood together admiring the car before the race.

"Sure is a shiny piece of equipment," Billy grinned. "Too bad it ain't gonna be in the winner's circle."

"Huh! What you talking about, boy," Bobby snorted. "I'll be in the winner's circle way before you ever get started good!"

They laughed and playfully punched each other on the arm. Billy was suddenly sober and looked deep into his brother's eyes. No words passed between the two, but they threw their arms around each other's shoulders and walked away from the car together. As they lined up for the lap behind the pace car, Bobby caught his brother's eye and threw him a salute and a grin. Billy returned the greeting to his baby brother.

Less than halfway into the race, there was a terrible crash on the upper turn, away from the stadium. Billy was just approaching the turn and saw it happen. It looked like an explosion with pieces of metal and glass and tires flying all over the track and infield. His heart jumped to his throat as he thought he recognized the bright, shiny Oldsmobile being driven by Bobby. It was in the midst of the melee.

Drivers began to pull off the track to get around the mayhem. Billy sped off the track, stopped in the infield and ran toward the chaos. Cars swerved and spun out in an attempt to miss him as he sprinted recklessly across the track. Drivers were crawling out of their wrecked vehicles as Billy approached. He felt as if he was moving in slow motion. His legs were like heavy logs as his brain screamed at them to move. He approached his brother and could see him slumped over the steering wheel, flames engulfing the car and Bobby.

"Bobby! Bobby!" he screamed as he tried to reach his brother.

Numerous strong arms stopped him cold. He struggled and kicked and screamed, trying to escape his captors. It was several minutes before he could be constrained. Fire extinguishers covered the burning car and Bobby with their white clouds but the gasoline was relentless.

"Stop it, Billy!" It was Tiny Lund, shouting to get his friend's attention. "Ain't nothing we can do, buddy. Ain't nothing we can do."

Billy sank to the ground, paralyzed by shock and grief, as he watched his brother's charred body sitting in the once-shiny race car. Billy Myers was never the same after that day. He, as the older brother, had always looked after little Bobby. He felt as if he had failed him somehow.

Many of his friends worried about Billy after that fateful day. He never raced with the same zealous abandonment and enthusiasm as before. Many times after a race at various tracks, he'd be sitting quietly with his friends as they laughed and talked about the day's events and failures and successes.

"I seen Bobby on the track today," was his frequent comment. "Right over there in turn three. Standing right by the edge of the track. Grinned and waved at me as I passed. He's watching out for me, I reckon. Like I couldn't do for him."

The group would fall silent whenever Billy would have that conversation with himself. Wasn't anything any of them could say so they would just sit with him. It seemed to give him comfort.

On April 12, 1958, the drivers converged on Spartanburg, S.C. for a day of racing. The weather was clear and the sun bright with just a faint nip in the early spring air. Over 72,000 screaming fans filled the stands, waiting to cheer on their favorite gladiator. The drivers greeted each other, slapping each other on the back, cracking jokes, sharing time together.

This ritual was a faithful part of their routine and was their unspoken way of wishing each other well and even saying goodbye, in case it came to that. Bill France made his customary visit with them, wishing them all well. Goodbye and love and respect didn't have to be verbalized for the group to know it was there.

"Let's run a clean race, fellas," France requested. "No fighting and no cutting off. You got that, Turner?"

"Why the hell you looking at me?" Curtis asked, feigning surprise.

The whole group laughed at the irony of Curtis's so-called statement of innocence. He was the original bad boy of racing and would fight anybody, even a spectator, anywhere, anytime, over anything, if given an excuse. France shook his head and smiled as his eyes moved across the group. He loved these men like brothers and would do anything he could to help them or to keep them safe.

"You doing okay, Billy?" His eyes stopped and rested kindly on Billy Myers.

"Yeah, Bill, I'm doing great. Ready to run."

His eyes stayed a moment longer on Billy before moving away.

"Okay, fellas, let's give the folks their money's worth and show 'em what they came to see!"

As the starter flag dropped, the crowd leaped to their feet, screaming with joy. The drivers were running well and the crowd loved it. Curtis Turner passed Billy Myers as they went around turn number two. Curtis glanced over toward Billy as he passed and was surprised to see Billy looking to his left.

What's he looking at? Curtis wondered, as he sped by.

Billy seemed to be slowing down. Curtis glanced into his rearview mirror and saw the car slowing down even more. Billy was drifting off the track.

Billy was feeling well that day, better than he had since Bobby had been killed. He had dreamed about Bobby the night before. Bobby seemed so real, like Billy could touch him. Bobby had walked up to his brother as he stood beside his race car, helmet in hand. Dressed in a suit, Bobby looked well.

"Hey, buddy, good to see ya."

"Yeah, good to see you too, brother. I sure do miss you," Billy responded.

"No need to fret. I'm doing great. And we'll be together soon enough."

Billy wanted to tell him how sorry he was he couldn't save him at Darlington, but Bobby just saluted him, winked and disappeared. He secured himself into the car and got ready to race. He was smiling and waving at all his racing buddies. They'd been real good friends to him these past seven months since Bobby died. Fact was, they'd always been good friends but most especially during the difficult days behind him. He moved expertly around the track, passing easily, the car running perfectly. He felt one with his machine and was not even dismayed when other drivers would pass him. As he started through turn number two a little more than halfway through the race, he saw somebody walking across the infield toward him.

Hey, that looks like Bobby! he thought.

He felt an urgency to get around the track and back to turn two, so he moved quickly, taking advantage of every opening. As he returned to that spot on the track on his next lap, he slowed down and started staring intently to his left, toward the infield. This time the figure didn't disappear.

"Hey, Bobby!" he yelled joyfully out the window. He pulled off the track, into the infield and came to a stop. He jumped out of the open window and ran toward his brother.

Funny, he thought, as he approached Bobby, *I don't even remember unbuckling my harness!*

He threw his arms around his smiling brother and greeted him warmly.

"Hey, buddy, I've missed you! How you been?"

"I'm great, Billy, and so are you now." He pointed back to the stopped car in the infield.

People were running toward the car and Billy looked in confusion as he saw someone slumped behind the steering wheel.

"Who..." he began.

Then he realized. He looked down at himself and then back at the car. It was him, slumped behind the wheel. But he was standing here.

"I'm dead, ain't I?"

"Not really, brother. This is just the beginning of a wonderful adventure." Bobby placed his arm over his brother's shoulder and led him gently away.

Speedy Thompson won the race that day in Spartanburg. He stood in the winner's circle, wondering about his buddy Billy Myers. The ambulance had come and Billy had been gently removed from his car and taken away to the hospital. There had been no announcement and everybody was gathered around in tight little groups, whispering and wondering. Speedy was happy to be in the winner's circle but his mood was also subdued. Even the crowd seemed quieter as they cheered for Speedy but worried about Billy. They really became uneasy as they watched Bill France approach the microphone, head down and a frown on his face.

"This don't look good," Speedy muttered to his crew standing beside him in Victory Lane.

"Ladies and gentlemen."

He waited for the crowd to quiet down before speaking again.

"We want to thank everybody for being here today, especially the drivers and their families. We're very happy for Speedy and his great win. It was a good, clean race."

He hesitated for a moment, searching for his words. The crowd remained still.

He cleared his throat. "I'm sorry to have to tell you that we lost a great young man today. Billy Myers died in turn number two, we think of a heart attack."

The crowd moaned. His voice broke and he struggled to regain his composure. "The doctors say they think that was for sure what killed him. We in the racing family loved Billy. And we loved his brother Bobby who was killed in Darlington last September. Billy was just 33 years old and Bobby was 30 when he died. Let's bow our heads in a moment of silent prayer for our brother Billy."

Some in the stands sobbed openly as they bowed their heads.

"It won't a heart attack that killed Billy. It was a broke heart," Curtis Turner commented as he removed his helmet and stood silently.

CHAPTER 7
Curtis Turner and Louise Smith, Rough and Tumble Drivers

Curtis Turner was the quintessential juvenile delinquent of early racing. He was a party boy from the get-go. Hard drinking, fast driving, fast women, reckless gambling, he did it all.

"Curtis just didn't care," Peewee Jones once observed. "He was just out to have a good time. He loved to party and he loved to race. He had a small plane and he flew just like he drove – wide open."

Curtis was from Roanoke, Virginia, and his racing career spanned 17 years. Even though he won very few sanctioned races during his career, he was one of the best known and best loved drivers to the fans. They loved and admired his spirit and his guts. He had no fear on or off the racetrack. He won hundreds of races during his career but many of them were outlaw races, unsanctioned, and thus not recognized by official records.

Bill France had the patience of Job with Curtis, always trying to shelter him and protect him, mostly from himself. It was as if France understood what made Curtis tick. Curtis was married to a lady named Lillie, and she bore him four children. There was, however, an illness that frequently sent Lillie to the hospital or the state mental institution through the years. Curtis would race and drink and gamble and fight, always with a pretty woman on his arm. A woman other than Lillie. He would be worse when she was ill and it was impossible to decide if Lillie was sick because of his wildness or if Curtis was wild because of her illness. At any rate, the children were the losers in their parents' struggles. Curtis would buy a new automobile with his winnings, he and Lillie would get into a fight about something, and she would take a hammer, breaking out every window in the car. He would drink even heavier, and have more women with him after these incidents. He also didn't know how to handle his money and was frequently destitute, no matter how much he won. So was his family.

Louise Smith, a woman racer, was, without reservation, the wildest woman race car driver ever, and even offered competition for wildness to some of the men. Her husband, who owned a car dealership, did not know she raced, and she would race anyone who would answer her challenge on the back roads of Greenville, S. C. She outran the local police on a weekly basis, and finally got the attention of Bill France. He gave her a chance to race in Greenville in 1946. She came in third at that first race, and Bill invited her to race at Daytona. She qualified at #13 on her maiden race in Daytona.

She would take cars from her husband's car dealership and have the mechanics modify them so she that could get more speed out of them. She crashed into a large pile of cars on one of the turns during her maiden race, crushing the top of her husband's brand new 1947 Ford. She had crashed into Curtis Turner's car, and when she crawled out of her damaged vehicle, she was furious. She ran to him, fighting mad and spitting fury, just as he was crawling out of his own dented and damaged car.

"Damn, you, Turner! You done wrecked Noah's brand new car and he's gonna kill me!"

"Hell, woman, you're crazy. I ain't wrecked no-damn-body!"

She swung her fist at him, connecting with his chin and knocking him back against his car.

"Hey!" he yelled, more surprised than hurt. He jumped toward her, grabbed her flailing arms and pinned them against her side.

She kicked his shin; he screamed in pain and shoved her away, causing her to fall to the ground. She immediately recovered, running back toward him with all the fury of an angry bull. He managed to raise his arms, diverting her blows to his shoulder and away from his face. Several drivers arrived and pulled her off, while Curtis regained his composure.

"Damn!" he gasped in total surprise. "I didn't know what the hell had a hold of me."

Soon the top of Louise's car was beaten out with a hammer so she could finish the race, but she later lamented, "I don't know what in the hell I'm gonna tell Noah about what happened to his car. He thinks I'm down here on vacation."

Louise would drink, cuss and fight just like the men. However, she never ran moonshine, but she rode with some who did run it, and she loved the speed and danger of outrunning the law.

The entire racing family was uneasy when Curtis bought a small twin-engine airplane to fly to and from races. They were terrified that he would get killed in that plane. They would watch him take off and they could hear him yelling, "Yeehaw!" as he sped down the runway. He was usually drunk or drinking heavily when he flew.

A car dealer, by the name of Malley from South Carolina, was a friend to Curtis. They would frequently sit in the car dealership after business hours and drink, laugh and talk, usually with a couple of women with them as well. Late one Saturday night (or early Sunday morning), the two ran out of liquor. The women with them had left already, and Malley lamented the fact that they were out of alcohol.

"Wish I'd brought along that jug of homebrew I got stashed in the basement," he whined.

"Hell, that ain't no problem!" Curtis declared. "We'll go get it! Haul your hind end into the plane and we'll just go get it!"

Soon the two were airborne, although it was a miracle they even got off the ground. The plane was parked at the small airport near the car dealership and Curtis ran it up the runway, and they were soon off the ground. His "Yeehaw!" echoed through the still darkness of the night. They bounced around in the sky for over an hour, trying to find landmarks. They began to get their bearings after daylight. The daylight coupled with the fact that they were beginning to sober up gave them some idea of what was below them.

Malley lived in a large bungalow, across the street from a small, white Baptist church. It was a country church but was right on the edge of town so it was relatively easy to pick out from the air, especially with the white steeple standing proud and tall. There were no instruments in the plane and Curtis didn't have a compass with him so he was searching for landmarks. He would fly dangerously low, trying to read street signs and company names on buildings, barely missing power lines and treetops.

They finally spotted the church and Malley's house across the street. Curtis made a sudden dip and prepared to land.

"Damn, Curtis, be careful," Malley snapped. He was now sober enough to be scared by the reckless flying and behavior of his friend. "I sure as hell don't wanta die over that jug of whiskey!"

"Hey, don't worry! I've got everything under control." Just as he made this statement, Curtis dropped with a thump onto the paved road approaching Malley's house. He slammed on the brakes, cut the engines and left a cloud of smoke from the burning asphalt in their wake. He slid into the dirt parking lot of the church across the street, bounced over the ruts, and ran parallel with the cemetery, nearly clipping headstones with his right wing. He spun it around, headed back to the parking lot and came to a stop just at the entrance.

Church members were arriving for Sunday school and ran, terrified, away from the attacker, scrambling to escape into the church. There were only a few cars parked near the church and that prevented the plane from crashing into them and causing even more damage. Malley jumped out of the plane, tore across the street into his house while Curtis waited impatiently. The engines were idling, causing the propellers to throw dust and dirt all around the church and the frightened parishioners. Suddenly their fear began to turn to anger and they began shouting and screaming at the pilot. One member had managed to get his car out of the parking lot and went speeding toward a service station several blocks up the street.

Bet he's going to call the law, Curtis thought, as he watched him drive away. He grinned mischievously, eager for a chase. He saw Malley run out his front door and across the yard.

"Hurry up, Malley," he screamed as he revved up the two engines, ready to explode out of the parking lot.

Malley arrived back at the plane and scrambled aboard, throwing the jug in first. Before he got his legs inside, Curtis was pulling across the parking lot. As the plane entered the road, he saw red lights flashing to his left in the far distance.

"Looks like the law's on its way," he shouted to Malley above the den of the engines. "We'll have to go to the right."

"That ain't good!" Malley observed. "That's downtown to the right and there's a traffic light down yonder at the intersection. Not more'n a half mile or so."

"No need to worry! That gives me plenty of room. Yeehaw!"

He gunned his engines and bounced down the narrow road. The church members ran into the parking lot and watched him in disbelief. He attempted to get the wheels off the road before approaching the intersection but it loomed ahead, the red traffic light gleaming at him like the eye of a demon.

"Oh, hell, we ain't gonna make it!" Malley screamed, clutching the dashboard of the plane in desperation. His knuckles were white and so was his face as he saw cars pulling through the intersection and turning in front of their path. "I can't believe I was stupid enough to get back in this damn plane with you! We ain't gonna make it, damn it!"

"Oh, yes, we are, buddy! You can count on me! Yeehaw!"

The sirens were screaming, coming closer and Curtis was getting more speed into his engines. His hand rested on the stick, ready to pull them up and over the cars ahead of them. Several of the people in the cars evidently saw a plane heading their way in their rearview mirrors and ran off the road, either in shock or in an attempt to get out of the way. Curtis sailed through the intersection, the light still red and lifted off the highway into the sky, just before the sheriff's deputies arrived at the intersection. He flew in a circle, waving down and laughing at the angry lawmen and frightened civilians.

"Yeehaw!" echoed across the fields and parking lots.

When the two landed at the Greenville Airport a little while later, law enforcement was waiting for them. They handcuffed Curtis and took him away. Malley got in his car, followed them down to the police station and bailed his buddy out. Curtis lost his flying license over that incident but it didn't seem to bother him much and certainly didn't calm him down. The next weekend, he was racing at Martinsville when his legendary anger flared.

As he came around one of the turns, he noticed a spectator standing up on the newly erected grandstand with something in his hand. As the cars drove by, a beer bottle from the hand of the man came bouncing across the track, barely missing several cars. Curtis tore around the track, cussing and muttering all the way. When he arrived back at the turn, he screeched to a stop beside the wall, leaped from his car, jumped onto the hood and up over the six-foot high fence between the track and the stands. He saw the man and charged at him with all the ferocity of an angry bull.

"You son-of-a-bitch, you coulda killed somebody with that damn bottle! I'm gonna whoop your ass!"

Bill France strained to see what was happening and when he saw that Curtis's car had pulled over and stopped, he moaned, ran his hand through his hair and screamed, "Get that flag out! Stop the race!"

Soon all the drivers were pulled to the side and several were climbing over the fence after Curtis, pulling him off the intoxicated fan. The fan was escorted out of the track and Curtis was told to report back to Bill France and get off the track. Curtis paid no attention to the directive and crawled back into his car, resuming the race. It took several laps for France to get him to pull over and when he did, France was livid. He jerked Curtis up out of the window of his car.

"That's it, Turner! You're through! You ain't gonna race no more for me or my company! Now get your sorry self off this track!"

Curtis left, looking much like a whipped puppy. He was fined a whopping $500 but he never paid the fine. A fine didn't bother him at all. He just wanted to race. After a couple of weeks, the fans made so much commotion, France had to bring him back to the tracks. Like him or not, Curtis was a big name draw that brought in the crowds and the money. It infuriated France that he had to put up with Curtis's errant behavior but it hurt him even more that he couldn't reach this troubled man.

Curtis continued to fly his plane and race his car, all with reckless abandonment and terrifying danger. He would buzz houses with his plane, yelling down to say hello to people he knew. He once buzzed a golf course where he knew the pro, causing the golfers to throw themselves onto the ground in fear for their lives. He ran moonshine before his career in racing really began and that's how he learned to drive a car so well. He would outrun law enforcement vehicles on a regular basis, loving to toy with and tease them.

It seemed the more frequent Lillie's illnesses, the more reckless Curtis's behavior. During her times of hospitalization, he would bring more and more women around, some of whom attempted to care for the children. Curtis and Lillie finally separated after one of her visits to the mental hospital. She was set up in a small house and Curtis paid child support each month. They divorced in December 1968, and he married Bunny Vance in January 1969.

Bunny seemed to have a taming effect on Curtis. He adored her and when he was not at home, he would call her every night. For the first time in his life, he was playing it straight. Bunny brought deep and abiding family values to the Turners, and was a loving influence on the children as well. Life for the children was reasonably stable and it appeared to be stable for Curtis as well.

When son Ross was 15 years old, he drifted off to sleep at his mother's home one night. His father and Clarence King were in Pennsylvania in Curtis's plane. As Ross fell asleep, he had a dream. In his dream, he saw a plane crash. He could see and feel the plane going down, and he awoke with a start. Realizing it was just a dream, he fell into a deeper sleep, only to be awakened around midnight by a knock at the door. Ross got up and answered the door. His mother was sitting motionless in a rocking chair, unable to muster the energy to move, much less answer the door. She was in another of her catatonic illness states. His sister stood on the other side of the door.

"What's the matter?" he asked, fear and dread gripping his heart.

"It's Dad, Ross," she spoke softly.

He stood there motionless, waiting for the words that would rip his heart out.

"His plane crashed today. He's gone."

Ross began screaming. He ran through the house screaming and crying, his mother making no movement toward, or acknowledgment of her son. He screamed constantly until nearly dawn, until he was hoarse, until he had no tears, no sounds, nothing left inside himself. He was a hollow shell, a shadow, a void.

On October 4, 1970, the party ended when Curtis Turner, racing legend, reformed bad boy, loving father and husband crashed his plane into a hill in Pennsylvania. And in some ways, so did the lives of many others, including his children. The 46-year-old Curtis did not leave a will, and everything went to his wife Bunny and their unborn child. Lillie was not able to care for the children much of the time as she was in and out of hospitals. The children were consequently in and out of orphanages or foster care in the years until they became adults.

In retrospect, it would appear to an outsider that Curtis Turner was an angry man with a death wish. Unable to cope with the pain of a mentally ill wife, he did everything he could to lose himself in his activities and his relationships. The double tragedy in his death is that he was beginning to find himself, to accept life on terms other than his own and to become a loving father to his children.

CHAPTER 8
Bill Blair, Jr., Jim Paschal and Billy Biscoe

Ernest Wood was a coal miner and also owned an Oldsmobile dealership in Corbin, Ky. He owned two race cars and hired Jimmie Lewallen and Jim Paschal to run them for him. The cars were kept in North Carolina since that's where both Lewallen and Paschal lived. Paschal's car was named Helz a-Poppin' and Lewallen's was Helz A-fire.

Jim Paschal rented a shop on Highway 68 on what is now Eastchester Drive in High Point and the two worked on their cars there. Bill Jr. helped them both as his dad had just about quit racing by then. It was 1955 and Bill Jr. was in high school and thrilled to be able to help them out. He was proud to be mechanic to Paschal and Lewallen.

Bill Jr. would ride to the races each weekend with Paschal and sometimes even during the week. School started after Labor Day, and many students in those years were needed at home to finish bringing in crops and clear the fields for the next year's crops so there was no problem with the schools if someone missed the first week or two of school. Bill Jr. was one who would miss those first days so that he could work at the racetracks with Paschal. Bill Jr. worked for Paschal throughout his high school career and idolized the driver. He learned much from Paschal, both about cars and life.

Paschal was a gentleman, an honest and a fair man. He had the reputation of being a clean driver and was probably one of the best ever. He seldom participated in fighting, but would stand up for himself should he be treated unfairly or with aggression. Bill Jr. was at home one night and had just finished his homework when his dad came in from work at the service station he operated.

"Paschal came by today," he shared with the family when he entered the kitchen.

Bill Jr. immediately looked up, curious to know what his father had to say about his hero.

"Paid his gas bill. Just like he always does. Jim Paschal is one of the most honest men I've ever known. Him owing you money is just like money in the bank. He always pays his debts. Gotta respect that in a man."

Bill Jr. made no comment but he smiled proudly to himself. His respect for Paschal was only intensified by observations and testimonies such as this. Jim Paschal had been in the Navy before Bill Jr. had met him. Jim was a strong, muscular, handsome man. The women were drawn to him and he frequently had a pretty woman on his arm.

One day, he met a petite beauty with dark eyes and long hair and he took notice of her at once. Her name was Becky Rich and there was a quality about her that touched him deeply. He learned that she had recently been divorced and had a 6-month-old son named Al. Many men in the late 1950s and early 1960s would have been put off by a ready-made family, but not Jim. He immediately connected with this woman and her tiny child. Jim, always a faithful and loyal friend, was equally faithful to his Becky and her son. So far as anyone knows, he never saw another woman after he started dating Becky, and he was as good a father to Al as any man could ever be. And Becky and Al adored him.

Becky wisely made no demands of her man as the years of their courtship passed. She was just glad to have him in their lives and concentrated on making him as happy as she possibly could. He was reluctant to marry, as he had seen so many marriages go bad in the racing family. He also didn't want to leave Becky a widow should he be killed on the racetrack.

Ford Motor Company sponsored Dick Hutchinson, a northern driver, in a car and brought him down from Michigan to race. He was intent on building a reputation and he had heard much about Jim Paschal's driving. And winning. He decided this would be the man he would use to prove himself. During a race at Martinsville, Dick stayed close to Jim for several laps, watching, waiting, sizing him up, learning to know his moves and habits. As they approached a turn, Dick eased up really close behind Jim and as they entered the turn, he shoved Jim's car with his front bumper. Jim spun out and slid sideways for several hundred feet before regaining control.

That race ended and Jim made no comment at all to Dick Hutchinson. Dick was acting very smug, thinking he had shown the others that he wasn't afraid to be aggressive. He thought that Jim must be afraid of him since he made no comment about the shove. As the next race started, Dick Hutchinson was feeling pretty cocky and sure of himself. He pulled up behind Jim, who pulled aside, allowing him to pass. Dick laughed and waved as he sped by and over in front of Jim's car. They reached the straightaway and he saw Jim rushing toward him. Before he had time to react, Jim's bumper slammed against his and Dick went flying over the fence. There was no time to think about it, and he was still in shock when he bounced to a standstill on the other side of the fence. Dick Hutchinson had a new respect for this driver Jim Paschal that he had mistakenly perceived as a pushover. He didn't bother Paschal again.

The drivers and their families knew from the get-go that someone could get hurt in these races. If there was a wreck, it was very tense, especially for the wives. Lucille Blair had quit going to the races because she was so worried about Bill Sr. She supported his wish to race but couldn't bear to be there should he be hurt, so she chose to stay at home. After sixteen years of being with Becky and Al, Jim Paschal realized that they were his family and nothing that could happen to him would hurt them anymore if he acknowledged that fact to the world. He had seen the other women worrying and knew that Becky worried the same as they did, even without dried ink on a marriage certificate. So it was then that he married his Becky, the one to whom he had always been faithful, the one to whom he would always be faithful.

Shortly after their marriage, Jim went into Al's room and sat down on the bed beside him. He placed his arm around the 16-year-old and said, "Son, me and your mama are married now, and I was wondering if you want me to adopt you so you can have the same last name as we do. It don't matter whether you have the same name or not, you'll always be my son."

"And you've always been my dad and always will be. Nothing ain't gonna change that. Won't that cost a bunch of money to get my name changed?" Al wondered.

"That don't matter none. If you want it done, it'll be done."

Al thought about it for a few minutes, but at the age of 16 his friends had known him as Al Rich forever, and he was reluctant to make that change to his last name.

"Naw, if it's okay with you, I'll just leave it like it is. That don't change nothing between us anyhow."

Jim threw his arm over Al's shoulder and assured him, "That's fine, Al, and no, it don't change nothing between us. You'll always be my son."

He smiled fondly at his son and left his room. Al Rich forever introduced Jim Paschal as his father. And so he was Al's father, in spirit, mind, soul and heart.

In the 1950s and early 1960s, it was the "in" thing for drivers to own their own private airplanes. They were realizing success and making money, and it was important to participate in as many races as possible. They knew they had to keep their names in front of the fickle public if they were to remain in the spotlight. They would also arrive at the racetracks less tired and better able to compete if they were in a plane, as they weren't worn out by driving around the country, many times pulling their race car behind them. By then, most had their own race cars and were no longer using the family vehicle. They also had people working for them that would take the cars to the various racetracks before a race.

Jim Paschal jumped on the bandwagon and decided to buy his own plane. He took flying lessons, received his pilot's license and purchased a small, twin-engine plane so as to navigate to and from races more quickly. He proudly stood beside his plane, wiping at imaginary dust on the wing, Becky and Al standing nearby. Al was very excited about this new mode of transportation but Becky was silent.

"Come on, you two, let's take her for a spin!" He smiled warmly at his family and eagerly waved them over to the plane.

The two climbed aboard and were soon airborne. There were no instruments showing where they were, so flying had to be done in mostly clear weather and daylight. It was common knowledge that the planes followed the highways from one racetrack to another so anyone wishing to see an airplane, which was a novelty in that era, had only to drive down highways 29 or 311 or 62 or some other busy highway and look up into the skies. This was especially true on the weekends and it was common to see people parked by the side of the road, yelling and waving at airplanes as they dipped low to see where they were.

"Wow! This is great!" Al exclaimed, his face beaming. He leaned over to peer out the small, cloudy window to catch a view of the ground speeding by beneath them.

"Look, Mama!" he shouted. "Those cars look like matchbox cars!"

Becky smiled weakly and cautiously peered out but made no comment. She slipped her arm securely around her son and rode silently until they landed.

"Didn't you like the ride, Becky?" Jim asked gently.

"Oh, yes, it was fine. A little scary but real exciting. I know you enjoy it and Al certainly did."

He smiled at the woman he loved so much and slipped his arm around her shoulder.

"No need to worry, honey. I'll be fine."

She smiled, visibly relieved by his assurance.

Jim was invited to drive in a race at Darlington one weekend so he hopped into his plane and took off. Becky and

Al stayed at home as Al had just started school and they didn't want his lessons disrupted by a trip to South Carolina. The car Jim was to drive was at the track and the owner had asked him to drive that weekend. There was one race on Friday night, two on Saturday and one on Sunday, and Jim stood to make quite a bit of money just for driving, even if he didn't win so he felt like he really wanted to go.

He arrived in Darlington, found a pay phone and called home to let them know he had arrived safely.

"Drive good, Jim!" Al directed.

"I will, son, I will. And I'll see you Monday morning."

"Aren't you coming home Sunday?"

"Yeah, but you'll be asleep when I get home."

"No, I won't. I'll wait for you."

Jim laughed. "Okay, son, I'll see you Sunday night."

The races went well and Jim came in second on the last race Saturday. It was cloudy Sunday morning and officials weren't sure they'd be able to finish the race but they started it just the same. The stands were filled with fans, paying fans, so the race went on.

They stopped the race once for nearly an hour as it began to drizzle. It didn't rain enough, however, to settle the dust so fans that had gotten damp from the drizzle soon resembled mud hens as red dust settled on their skin and clothes. The ones wearing glasses had the outline of them on their faces and older fans with wrinkles had red dirt caught in the lines on their faces. There were even outlines of their rear ends on the bleachers where they sat. Some outlines were more distinct than others, as many stood up, screaming and shouting their excitement, through much of the race.

It had been a hard weekend, especially with the rain delay, so the drivers were anxious to get home. Jim looked up at the sky and decided he could climb above the low hanging clouds and make it home without too much delay. He had a small compass in his pocket and could use that to find the general direction back toward High Point.

He climbed into his plane and was soon airborne. He lined up with Highway 29 heading north and climbed above the clouds, keeping an eye on his compass. He flew for a couple of hours, the period of time it normally took to get back into North Carolina. He figured he was probably pretty close to, if not over, Charlotte by then. He carefully slipped through the clouds so as to get a better view of the road below him. He saw a town below him but thought it looked kind of small to be Charlotte so he dropped a little lower for a better look. He saw a neon sign on a small store near the edge of the highway and strained to read it through the light mist.

Rock Hill Stop and Shop, it read.

"Damn!" he muttered aloud. He was still in South Carolina. He had been flying into a heavy headwind and had miscalculated his progress. Area radio stations and buildings over three stories high had learned to place flashing lights on top so as to warn these low flying machines of their presence so he climbed above one looming ahead and resumed his trip. He would slip below the clouds about every fifteen minutes to make certain he was making progress. He didn't want to end up back in Darlington or on some small airfield or cornfield in South Carolina.

He made it home safely and landed at the small airfield on Beacon Light Road in north High Point at nearly midnight. He had followed city streetlights and car lights on the highway to get there so he was very glad to see the field. The owner had heard his plane and turned on a beacon light on the small tower at the end of the field. He pulled his car up on the side and aimed the headlights on the airstrip to light Jim's path. This was an agreement he had with the men who used his field and they knew right where his car would be so they could line up correctly with the landing runway.

Jim arrived home a short time later to a warm welcome and a house fully lighted. Al was on the sofa, nodding off in spite of his determination to remain awake, and when he heard the car, he sprang to life, rushing to the side door where he knew Jim would enter. It was difficult to know who was more relieved that night – Becky or Al, but Jim didn't bother to tell either of them about his adventure in getting home. Later that week, though, he decided that he would just sell his plane.

"It's getting to be too much of a big expense," he explained to Becky.

She really didn't care what reason he had, she was just secretly glad he had made that wise decision, but she kept her thoughts to herself. She supported Jim in whatever he wanted to do, as she trusted him completely to make the right and responsible decision. It never occurred to her to question his judgment or complain about his plans. And so, before long, Jim Paschal sold his plane and was out of the flying business, both feet firmly planted on the ground and in his race car.

After high school, Bill Blair, Jr. concentrated more and more on building racing engines. He had a great talent for his chosen vocation and soon was well known and respected for this gift of making an engine that could outrun many others. The power and purr of these mighty machines was nearly a religious experience for the drivers as they sat behind the wheel. They were humbled by the strength and speed created by these engines but proud to be able to control and direct the machines holding this power. They became one with the vehicle, just them against the elements and the other drivers. It created an intensely exciting and rewarding feeling of conquest and accomplishment to successfully navigate this beast of energy around a circle of red dirt and dust, the roar of the motor and the crowds filling their ears, echoing off ones ribcage, racing through the heart and reaching into the soul.

Bill Jr. became one with the motors he so lovingly and carefully built, knowing that they were not only the tool with which a driver could win a race but were also the destiny of that driver's safety and well being. He loved to stand aside and watch this creation of his propel a car and driver around a track, hurdling them through the race, fast, efficient and, best of all, safe. No one wanted to build an engine that would blow up in the middle of a race, losing the event and also putting the driver and all other drivers in danger as oil and debris spewed out onto the tracks.

Building these engines was serious business and something that Bill Jr. took literally to heart. Consequently, he became a much respected, honored and sought after creator of racing motors. Much more than a chosen career, his became a mission, a calling.

Billy Biscoe remained enamored with racing after he graduated from high school. The country was deep into the controversial Vietnam War, and his parents wanted him to enlist. Billy had no desire to enlist but finally followed the pressure placed on him by his parents. In 1969, he enlisted into the Army and was sent to the basic training. While there, he became known as a "ground pounder." Unable to conform to the rigors and discipline of Army life, he was constantly hearing, "Give me 50, soldier; give me 25, soldier." He would smart off at a superior and would once again find himself on the ground, doing pushups.

He completed basic training, probably still holding the

record for the number of pushups completed by a recruit, and was placed on a C147 to San Diego. He received all his shots and papers to be sent into combat in Vietnam. As he stood, ready to board the ship and face his destiny, he was pulled out of line. *Wonder what I did wrong this time?* he wondered. His medical records from basic training had caught up with him and there seemed to be some problem with his hands. There was some sort of numbness and slight paralysis in them, possibly from nerve damage caused by racing and fighting with the steering wheels and other drivers since the age of 15. At any rate, he was sent back to Florida and home.

Billy worked for his dad at the funeral home, making a little beer money, but he had no serious job. His buddies from high school were coming home from Vietnam in body bags, and he was helping to bury them. He felt he was burying every young man he ever knew. Billy was drinking more and more. The stress and pain of burying so many of his young friends had more of an adverse effect on him than even he realized at the time. Finally, one day he decided he'd better find a job away from the funeral home so he made his way to Daytona. He moved around the garages at the Daytona Motor Speedway, talking to any of the drivers and their crew that he could find. He approached Bobby Allison's area where work was being done on number 22.

"Mr. Allison?" Billy spoke with respect as he approached this well-known and honored driver.

"Yeah, kid, what can I do for you?" Bobby turned to Billy, wiping oil and grease off his hands onto a rag.

"I was just wondering if you could use some help. I know a lot about engines and have my own race car back in Tampa. I built it myself and been running it for a couple years. I sure would be honored to help you out."

Bobby smiled at the young man standing in front of him, trying not to laugh, as he looked him over. The kid couldn't be 20 yet so he doubted if he had too much experience. He probably had a midget car with a lawn mower engine on it. As he choked back his laughter, he spoke kindly to Billy.

"You couldn't 'a been running too long, kid. How old are you?"

"I'm 19, Mr. Allison, and I ran my first race when I was 15. Won too, but they wouldn't give me no money on accounta I was so young and all. But I built my own race car when I was 16 and I been running races nearly every weekend since. 'Cept when I was in basic training. I know how to race and I know about engines."

Allison wasn't convinced, but he liked this kid's nerve.

"I tell you what, kid. If you really want to work, we can use you to roll tires and help the pit crew out. That is, if you're interested."

"Oh, yes, sir, I'm interested."

"Okay, speed week starts this weekend so you be here on Saturday morning and you can help out."

"I'll be here, Mr. Allison, you can count on that." Billy couldn't hide his excitement and enthusiasm and Bobby smiled kindly in his direction.

"And, kid, the name is Bobby."

"Thank you, Mr. ...ah...Bobby." Billy smiled back as he continued to stand and watch. Soon he was helping push the car, bringing rags for the crew to clean the engine and themselves, picking up cigarette butts and empty coffee cups, anything to be useful and just to be with the racing people he admired so much. He couldn't wait until Saturday to start.

He worked hard and with great dedication, doing any menial job that needed to be done. He never complained and was always on time. He quickly gained the respect of Bobby Allison and his whole crew, and they also soon learned that he truly did know about engines.

"Billy, we're through with you here but we could sure use you again if you're interested," Bobby explained. Speed week had ended but they liked the work this talented young man did for them so he would follow them around, doing all that he could to help. He was paid in cash and drank it all up but he was with the racing community, and he was happy.

He eventually found himself in North Carolina and was hired by Petty Enterprises at Level Cross. The Pettys were very good to Billy and he, in turn, did great work for them on their engines. In addition, he would race most weekends at Hickory and Carraway. He was living in Denton, met a local girl, married and they had a son. He was completely engrossed in working at Petty Enterprises and racing. Every penny he made went back into his race car, which he kept in the basement of their home.

One night, the pangs of hunger sent him upstairs, away from his work in the basement.

"What's for supper?" he asked as he entered the kitchen.

His wife burst into tears.

"You haven't given me any money in two weeks and there's no food here," she sobbed.

He stood in shock and shame, turned, went down to the basement, turned off the lights and came back upstairs. He reached into his pocket and pulled all the money he had out, laid it on the counter and said, "Here, let's go get something to eat."

Billy had been winning many races, but he was putting nothing back to support the family or pay the bills. He took his paycheck from the Pettys and put every nickel of it on his race car.

He looked at his wife and promised, "I ain't never gonna race again, I promise you that."

It was, unfortunately, too late. He lost his wife, his son and his home. He did not, however, forget his promise, a promise to himself as much as to his now lost wife. True to his word, Billy Biscoe never raced again. He continued to build racers for others to drive and he restored old race cars for museums but he never again climbed behind the steering wheel of a race car to run a race.

As he worked with the Pettys, he was given the opportunity to work with some of the Chrysler engineers so he learned a great deal through his connections with the legendary family. He wanted to work for himself and he established his own Saturday night speed shop that he operated for over 11 years. He attended over 850 short track races selling parts and advice to Saturday night racers.

Billy made a commitment to his customers that he would make their car better. There was no guarantee that they would win, but he could promise that their car would be better. Many times the advice was free, just so he could help someone.

"You can't put a price on winning, you can't buy a win," Billy explained to someone seeking advice. "You have to learn how to win and many people don't understand that. Many of today's racers think with all their megabucks, they can buy a win. All you can do is buy the parts. You can't win it unless you know how.

"I would drive a car so that I could relate as a crew chief what was happening to the car. I would have that feel of how it would react on the speedway. When they came back and talked to me about that twitch or that wiggle, I could relate to it and help fix it. Having experience driving my own cars and winning was an asset so I could relate their problems to my own experience."

Billy's son, A.J., had a desire to race so Billy built a race car for him. The car was an overkill on the roll bars and driver protection and an attempt was made to teach A. J. safety. A. J. would have no part of it. A.J. was in a lower division of racing with four cylinder motors. His first race was a ten-lap race; five in one direction and then five in the other direction, at Caraway Racetrack in Randolph County, North Carolina.

"Now, son, when you go out on that racetrack, just be careful. Watch the other cars, stay out of their way, be careful passing and don't take no stupid chances. You can win but the important thing is to run safe. Don't hurt nobody and don't get hurt yourself." Billy shook his head, his brow furrowed with concern, as he realized A. J. was not listening.

As soon as the flag dropped, 21-year-old A. J. Biscoe screamed away from the starting line. He ran like a bull in a china shop, crashing into the rear of the pace car as it attempted to get out of his way. He barely noticed that he had hit anything, and soon he sideswiped a car as he passed it.

There were a total of six race cars in the race, and as A.J. finished the first five laps, he began to make his turn for remaining laps. He crashed and bumped into all five of the other cars, including the one he had sideswiped earlier, as he was turning around. He even hit a post supporting the fence as his rear end fish tailed after completing his turn. By the end of the race, he had collided with everything on the track except the fire truck and the ambulance. It was a total train wreck.

He didn't win that race, but needless to say, he caught the attention of the fans, other drivers and the racing officials.

"Son, this ain't no demolition derby," Billy admonished. "What you trying to do, get killed?"

A.J. did go on to win many races and was moved up a class on the tracks, but he sold his car, wasted all the money he had won, got married and then divorced.

"The apple don't fall far from the tree," Billy remarked quietly to a friend.

Bill France, Sr., if he were alive, would probably say today, "I took a band of troublemakers and organized them."

Drivers included many thieves, or liquor runners, or con artists, most on the edge, even over the edge, of being legal.

Most had no earned income, as working a full-time job was too constraining for their racing. There simply wasn't time to work in a furniture factory or cotton mill and have a race car because they had to work on the race car all the time.

"We put our soul into it," Billy Biscoe stated with affirmation. "Those who had a job and just raced on the weekends didn't accomplish too much. They didn't end up winners. Once in awhile they'd get lucky and win but if you were a race car driver as an occupation, that's what you did 24/7. We ran moonshine to get money to work on the cars.

"There was a man down in Seagrove who had two cars, one a two-door and one a four-door, and I wanted to buy them. He told me he'd sell them both to me, but he wouldn't give me the title to the four-door because he was using it to run liquor and he was afraid the law was looking for it. I didn't insist because the paperwork didn't mean anything to me because I was only interested in the parts. The two-door was his family car and the four-door was his money making car."

This dedication and even obsession with the sport of racing marked the beginning of an empire unsurpassed in today's world. It was built on the blood, sweat, pain, sacrifice, misery and tears of early drivers, their wives, their children and their friends. They were an impassioned group unable to see or comprehend or accept anything beyond their love of racing.

In 1999, the years of hard living and harder drinking finally caught up with Billy Biscoe. He suffered a major stroke and it was thought that he would be in a wheelchair for the rest of his life. The medical community, however, was not intimately familiar with the spirit and determination of this independent man.

Billy spent 36 days in a wheelchair. While in that chair, he made a conscious decision not to be a burden to his family. He would rather not be alive than to be a burden so he concentrated all his energy and thoughts into leaving that wheelchair. And so he did. His speech remains halting and his gait is slower but he is ambulatory and perfectly capable of communicating. He admits that some of his memories are gone but many more remain. His mind and his memory are walking, talking histories of the racing sport, and he remains a valuable American treasure.

CHAPTER 9
Monkey on the Back

Drivers were always looking for a gimmick or something to make them more visible to the fans. Thus they began painting their cars bright, outrageous colors, or designed and wore gaudy, flashy uniforms. Their main focus was bringing attention to themselves.

Tim Ferguson from Atlanta was slated to be champion in 1952, his first national title, and was running his last qualifying race for this honor in W. Palm Beach, Florida. He did not have to win the race, and didn't even have to finish it in order to be declared champion. He only had to start in order to have enough points to qualify as the champion, as he already had 194 points. It took 200 points to win and he would earn 12 points just for starting the race in Florida that day.

He was running at W. Palm and doing quite well when an axle broke on lap 164. It was near the end of the race and the broken axle caused his car to turn over. He was sliding down the track, hood first, for several hundred yards and came to a stop in that position. He sat in his upside down car, stunned but conscious, his hands still gripping the steering wheel. His lap belt, the only safety equipment available in early race cars to secure drivers, was still hooked around his waist. He checked to make certain he wasn't injured, and he didn't seem to be. He released the lap belt and crashed into the inside roof as he waited for the rescuers to arrive.

"Damn," he muttered, struggling to right himself and angry about hitting his head as he smacked the roof. His helmet gave him protection, but he still sprained his neck in the impact.

Soon two men from different ambulance companies arrived, each eager to extricate the new champion from his car.

"You all right, Mr. Ferguson?" one inquired anxiously.

"Here, let me get you out of there, Mr. Ferguson," the other offered.

"Get out of the way, Fool. I got here first, I'm gonna get him out!" the other argued.

"Whatya mean, you got here first? You're nuts! I was here first, I'm gonna get him out!"

They started pushing and shoving each other, completely oblivious to Tim still trapped in the car. He stared in disbelief as they argued over who was going to take him to the hospital.

"Hey!" Tim yelled at the two standing by his car, "Quit your fightin' and get me outta this damn car! What's the matter with you two?"

They turned, with surprise on their faces, his voice bringing them back to what they were there for.

"Oh, sorry, Mr. Ferguson, I'm so sorry! It's just that I ain't never taken a National Champion to the hospital before," one apologized profusely and with obvious embarrassment.

"Me, too, Mr. Ferguson, I'll get you out of there."

"Don't worry about no National Championship right now, just somebody get me outta here!"

The two scowled at each other as they reached inside the car to remove Tim.

They pulled him gingerly out of the overturned vehicle, careful to make sure his legs were not caught.

"Are you okay, Mr. Ferguson?"

"Yeah, I think so, no thanks to you two," he grumbled.

He was a bit shaky and they placed him carefully on one of the stretchers lying on the ground. Other rescuers ran up to assist in carrying the stretcher into the ambulance that had arrived on scene. Tim waved to the fans as they moved him toward the ambulance and the entire crowd stood, cheering and applauding the new National Racing Champion. They were jubilant about the championship, as well as relieved that he was obviously not injured. He was checked out at the local hospital and returned to the track by the end of the race, much to the relief of his fellow drivers and the spectators.

Herb Thomas won the race that day but Tim was declared the 1952 Racing Champion and was the first driver to slide into the championship on his head and upside down. It didn't matter how he did it, he was still the undisputed champion that year. Tim adopted a tiny spider monkey in 1953 as his co-pilot. The small Rhesus monkey was a gift from Ted Chester of Atlanta, owner of Tim's race car. Ted saw him in a pet shop, and the monkey's name was Frederick. He thought that would be a good mascot for Tim and could be called Frederick Ferguson. Frederick quickly became famous around the racing circuit as Tim's racing partner.

Tim had Frederick riding on his back during the first race they ran together. Frederick jumped off his back and was looking out the passenger side window, curious as to what was going on. As Tim passed a driver on the track, the driver glanced over, saw the tiny monkey face peering at him, and nearly wrecked. No one knew about the monkey, as this bit of information was not shared with the NASCAR officials, until he was spotted, riding calmly in the front seat beside Tim or sitting on Tim's back. Tim was winning the race but had to actually pull over to get the monkey off his back so he could cross the finish line unobstructed. The monkey had become excited and was grasping his master's head, blocking his view of the track in front.

After the race, Junior Johnson, the surprised driver who had nearly wrecked, approached Tim. "Who the hell was driving that car, Ferguson? I knew you was ugly but I didn't think you was that ugly!"

They laughed as all the drivers gathered around to see this unusual competitor. NASCAR allowed Tim to run with the monkey as it brought in a great deal of attention and publicity to the sport. People, especially children, were very excited about Frederick. Tim had a uniform and helmet made for Frederick and installed a small seat in the passenger side so the monkey could be strapped in. Tim decided it was too distracting and dangerous to have him running around free in the car during a race. The posters began advertising Tim Ferguson and Frederick as racing partners and people gathered eagerly around Tim's car to catch a view of the monkey. Before each race, Frederick, dressed in his uniform and helmet, was strapped into his seat beside Tim and the crowd loved it. They would be cheering and screaming "Frederick! Frederick!" as the race started and each time Tim's car came around the track.

The cars of that era had a chain-operated panel in the floorboard that allowed the driver to peer beneath the car and check the tires. The chain would be pulled, the panel would open and the driver would glance quickly at the tires to determine if there was any problem so that a pit stop could be made before disaster struck. Frederick, always curious, would watch Tim open this panel. Somehow, Frederick managed to wiggle out of his safety strap during a race. Tim was busy and did not notice him until suddenly, Frederick pulled on the chain attached to the floor panel and the panel popped open. As he peered down at the dirt track speeding beneath the wheels, a small gravel flew up into the car and struck Frederick in the head.

"Frederick! No! Get back!" Tim yelled at his little companion, but it was too late. He picked Frederick up, laid him on the seat, and pulled into his pit as soon as he got back around to it.

"Take care of Frederick! He got knocked out! He opened the tire panel!" Tim handed his friend out the window as he sped back out onto the track. He worried all the way through the rest of the race until he could find out if Frederick was hurt.

One of his crew left the track as soon as Tim handed off Frederick and took the animal to a veterinarian near the racetrack. When the race ended, Tim jumped from his car.

"How's Frederick?" he asked anxiously.

"Where's Frederick? Where's the monkey?" The crowd was straining to see, anxious to catch sight of the small animal.

"He got tired and I took him out of the race," Tim explained as he hurried to check on Frederick.

He entered the veterinarian's office, still in his racing uniform, and was taken back immediately to speak to the doctor.

"I'm afraid he has a concussion, Mr. Ferguson," the doctor explained sadly. "It doesn't look good for him at this point. He's not regained consciousness and it would be my recommendation to put him down. With a serious head injury like this, he won't ever recover, even if he regains consciousness. I'm so sorry."

"Okay, Doc, I appreciate it." Tim was visibly shaken and upset by this injury to his friend. "Go ahead and do what you have to do. I don't want him to suffer."

Tim Ferguson and Frederick Ferguson had run only seven races together but the two had become legendary with the crowds. Tim dreaded facing the kids at the next race, as there was always a crowd of them around, waiting to see and pet Frederick.

The next weekend as he prepared to run in Atlanta, a group of children approached, just as he had feared.

"Where's Frederick, Mr. Ferguson?"

"Where's the monkey?"

"I'm sorry, kids, but Frederick got hurt and he died," he explained as kindly as he could.

The children immediately burst into tears and howls of pain. Tim felt terrible and worried about it throughout the entire race. He paced the floor at home after the race, running his hand through his hair.

"The kids cried, Frankie, when I told them Frederick is dead. What am I gonna do?" He was distraught as he spoke to his wife.

"Tim, you gotta come up with something else, some other reason the monkey isn't with you," she stated.

Finally, he stopped, his face lighting up.

"I know," he said, "I'll tell them I had to fire him because he wouldn't listen to me! That's what I'll tell them."

And that is exactly what he did in his future races. As the children approached and asked about Frederick, he would explain, "I had to fire that little booger. He just wouldn't follow orders and listen to me!"

The kids would laugh with delight at this explanation and the fate of Frederick became a well-guarded secret on the racing circuit.

Drivers were very suspicious and were careful not to breach what they viewed as a threat to their safety or luck. These daring young drivers took no chances with bad luck and omens and did everything possible to protect themselves against the unseen forces of fate and superstition. Fighting the cars and tracks they could see was one thing, but fighting the invisible terrified them and they obeyed these unwritten restrictions to the letter and faithfully.

At a race in Martinsville on a September Sunday, Jimmie Lewallen and Floyd Ferguson, Tim's brother, had an argument about Floyd's clothing. Floyd was wearing a pair of green pants with a black stripe down the side.

"Floyd, you got no business wearing them green pants," Jimmie accused. "You know green is bad luck out here on the racetrack."

"Don't worry about it, Lew. It's just a damn pair of pants. You just worry about your driving," Floyd answered.

"Just stay the hell away from me, Ferguson, that's all I gotta say," Jimmie glowered darkly at his competition.

That's all the incentive Floyd needed. They were fighting each other with their cars on the track from the start of the race. One would nudge the other and then the tables would be turned. It was that way throughout the entire race until finally, Floyd tapped Jimmie's driver's side fender in the back, sending Jimmie over and over five times.

Jimmie was pulled from his car and taken to the field hospital to be checked over. He was lying there, fuming and cussing to anyone that would listen about Floyd Ferguson and his green pants.

"Lay still, Mr. Lewallen," the ambulance attendant directed. "I need to get this glass pulled out of your hair and your neck."

Jimmie was still muttering when the doors burst open and another stretcher entered the room.

"Well, well, well," Jimmie sneered, "look what the cat drug up."

Floyd was lying on the stretcher, glass and blood trickling down his face. His green pants were muddy and both knees were torn out. He was more angry than hurt and the two men began cussing and yelling at each other as they lay there in the hospital, flat on their backs, with medical people attempting to clean them up so as to determine if there were any serious injuries.

"I told you, you S.O.B, not to wear them damn green pants! If you weren't so stubborn, my car wouldn't be tore up and I reckon from the looks of things, yours is tore up, too. Serves you right, you stubborn fool."

"Be quiet, Lew. You don't know what the hell you're talking about. I oughta get off this stretcher and beat your ass."

Jimmie pulled himself up, struggling to get up.

"Come on, big mouth. Let's see what you got! I can take you with one hand tied behind my back!" Jimmie was flailing, struggling against the men holding him down.

"Get Mr. Ferguson out of here!" a doctor shouted. "You two need to settle down or I'm gonna kick both of you out! We need to see if either of you is badly injured."

"He's too damn stupid to be hurt," Jimmie muttered menacingly.

The two glowered and scowled at each other as Floyd's stretcher was carried into an adjoining room.

The medical people continued working with Jimmie, pulling his shoes off to remove the glass stuck in his legs. Jimmie looked down as his shoes were removed.

"Oh, no," he moaned. There on his feet was a pair of green socks. He had dressed in the dark that morning and thought he had put black socks on.

"I gotta go talk to, Floyd, Doc. Seems I got some crow to eat," Jimmie said sheepishly.

CHAPTER 10
Fireball Roberts and Ned Jarrett

Glenn Roberts lived in Atlanta and was a natural born sportsman. He had the talent, dedication and brute strength needed to play sports and be successful at it. He was also an intelligent man and kept a cool head on his shoulders. He played baseball in Atlanta and became well known there as a very good pitcher. During his career playing baseball, he was nicknamed Fireball because of the speed of the fastball he would hurl. That nickname would stay with him throughout his lifetime and most people were not even aware that his given name was Glenn.

He became interested in racing as he attended some of the Atlanta races. He knew Smokey Yunick was an owner of race cars so he approached him to see if Smokey would hire him to drive. Smokey knew Fireball by reputation as a good baseball player and was happy to try him as a driver. Smokey was also very proud and particular about his cars and didn't like for anything to go wrong with them. He took it as a personal failure should a car break down during a race and fired many drivers through the years for blaming their losses on the car.

In 1959, Fireball was driving one of Smokey's cars at the Daytona 500. Near the end of the race, the engine blew up, putting Fireball and the car out of the race. As the car was towed back into the pit area, the media descended on Fireball.

"What happened, Fireball?"

Fireball, familiar with Smokey's sensitivity about the quality of his cars, thought quickly and carefully.

"Wellll," he began, "seems the starter fell off and hit the oil pan, causing the engine to burn up."

Mechanics and others standing around stifled smiles and grins as they realized what Fireball was doing. They all knew that this didn't likely happen, but none of them dared dispute the comments.

The media faithfully wrote it all down for publication the next day in their papers, and Fireball's loyalty to the owner of his car only increased the respect his peers held for this man. Racing inspectors were beginning to take a more serious look at race cars in the late 1950s to make certain nothing illegal was being installed so as to give a driver an unfair advantage. There were certain things that could be done to make a car run faster, and Fireball Roberts had the talent to drive these fast cars. He consequently became very hard to beat on the racetracks around the country.

Fireball became one of the first true superstars of stockcar racing. He was a very classy individual and great athlete. He was the first driver to display athletic ability in driving a race car. It was questioned for many years whether driving a stockcar was actually a sport or just a performance and whether these drivers were sportsmen or entertainers. Fireball, however, exemplified what was needed to be a good athlete and contributed much in making it a respected sport.

An inspection in Daytona of one of Smokey's cars Fireball was scheduled to drive found an illegal modification to the gas tank. The tank was pulled from the car and Smokey was notified.

"Mr. Yunick, you'll hafta put on another tank or we can't allow you to run. This gives you an unfair advantage over the other cars and it's against the rules."

Smokey was livid as well as embarrassed at being caught with his hand in the cookie jar. He sputtered and cussed and argued with the inspectors but to no avail.

"Hell, I'll just take my car and go home," he shouted as he jumped into his car, slamming the door behind him.

The motor started and he squealed out of the racetrack, throwing dust and gravel as he went. He traveled several miles to his home before it dawned on him that his gas tank had been pulled and he shouldn't have been able to drive away. He was chagrined and further embarrassed as he realized that he was caught once again. It wouldn't take a rocket scientist to figure out that he had another gas tank hidden somewhere on that car.

Guess I shoulda just kept my mouth shut, he thought, as he walked around his parked car, the one without a gas tank, the same parked car that had brought him home from the track with no problem of running out of gas.

Gentleman Ned Jarrett began his racing career in 1953. He was a quiet, laid back man who was not overtly aggressive, but he was no pushover and was well respected by drivers, owners and the media as well. He ran with all the greats including Fireball Roberts and Jim Paschal and he never felt obligated to spin out, or attack either of these friends on the racetrack. If there was a run-in or collision, it was understood by all three that it was probably an accident and there was no need for retaliation. A spin out would be a point of principle made by a driver who had been deliberately wrecked by another, and these early drivers could do things the current drivers can't do today. There wasn't the media coverage dramatizing every incident as they do today and NASCAR ignored many of those confrontations. It was felt that most of these theatrics were good for the sport.

One year in the early '50s, Bruton Smith was sponsoring a Grand National race at the Charlotte Fairgrounds. Curtis Turner and Buck Baker had gotten into a very big and serious fight, spinning each other out and fighting physically both on and off the track. Both threatened to get even with the other. Bruton Smith watched the confrontation with great glee and had an idea to capitalize on their feud.

There was no race scheduled for the next weekend in Charlotte, but Bruton called NASCAR, told them of the fight and asked for permission to schedule a grudge race. It was built up that way in the papers and on the radio for the whole week and brought in a large crowd the next weekend. It was Bruton Smith's nature to take advantage of arguments and fights so as to promote the races, and he loved that kind of rivalry. This sort of promotion was paramount in giving the races a reputation of being redneck brawls and hillbilly riots.

On race day, Turner and Baker were at the track, ready to race. A newsman sought the two out before race time.

"Curtis, do you think you'll have any trouble outrunning Buck today?"

"Hell, no, I ain't gonna have no trouble with that one. He ain't much of a driver anyway, and I got my eye on him. He spun me out twice last week and if he tries it again, he's gonna get hurt real bad."

Buck Baker walked up as the two talked. As he heard Curtis' remarks, he grabbed him by the arm and spun him around.

"Let's see you put your money where your mouth is, Turner," he growled.

Curtis jerked his arm away and swung his right fist, connecting with Baker's jaw. The two were soon rolling around on the ground, Bruton Smith standing nearby, grinning with delight. Crowds of people came running and the two were surrounded as they fought and scrapped. Several men in the crowd reached into their pockets, making wagers on which would win.

Bill France had arrived at the track, curious to see why this unscheduled race had been set. He saw the crowd, went over to investigate, and pushed his way to the center. He moaned as he saw Turner and Baker fighting. He ran over, pulling and pushing, attempting to separate the two.

"Cut it out!" he yelled. "That's enough. Leave each other be!"

The two men stood there, panting, blood splattered on their shirts, their hair wet with sweat, glaring and glowering at each other.

"This ain't no way to behave and I'm not gonna put up with it. Either you shake hands and run a clean race or both of you get the hell off this track!"

The crowd stood silently, waiting to see what would happen. The respect for Bill France was obvious as the drama played out. Finally, Buck Baker reached his right hand out tentatively toward Curtis Turner. Turner continued to glare for several seconds, but finally reluctantly took Baker's hand in a quick and half-hearted handshake. The crowd erupted into cheers and disbanded to return to their seats. The race itself was uneventful but Bill France had a private meeting with Bruton Smith during the running. No one knew exactly what transpired between the two but Bruton was very quiet during the rest of the race. He was no longer smiling. When approached by a newsman, he turned away, replying curtly, "No comment."

Ned Jarrett and Jim Paschal, also running in that race, both had a hearty respect for each other and they never had a serious run-in. Jim was very smooth and calculating and neither he nor Ned vented their feelings like the other drivers. They were clean racers.

Jim was asked by a news reporter, "What do you think about Ned Jarrett being labeled Gentleman Ned?"

"Yeah, he's a nice guy, but you get him on the back of some of these dark dirt tracks, you'll find out how much of a gentleman he is," Jim smiled.

"What do you mean, Mr. Paschal?" the reporter asked, pressing for more information.

Jim just smiled, turned and walked away. Ned was standing nearby and the two shared a knowing glance. There was mutual respect between the two, but each knew that one would not hesitate to take out the other should the need arise. It never did, however, throughout both their careers.

In 1958, Ned was running in the Sportsman Series in Richmond, Virginia. It was September and there were two more races in Greensboro that night. He wanted to make those races, but didn't see how he could if he raced in Richmond in the afternoon. There were no interstates at that time, only narrow and curvy, mostly unpaved roads so traveling from Richmond, Virginia to Greensboro, N. C. was pretty much a whole day drive. Eddie Newsome, a car dealer in Hickory and friend of Ned's, offered to fly Ned to Virginia and then to Greensboro in Eddie's private plane.

"Yeah, thanks, Eddie, that's great. It'll be a big help to me and I sure do appreciate it," Ned was relieved to be able to make both racetracks.

They arrived in Richmond and got to the racetrack early. Ned was driving a car owned by Smokey Yunick and won that race in an uneventful run. However, as the race ended, it was beginning to get very cloudy. Eddie had flown his plane low on the flight up, following the highways, and he watched the sky with a worried frown as they rode toward the airport. By the time the men reached the small airport in Richmond, it was raining. The owner of the airport came out to speak to them.

"It's okay, fellas, the weather is clear after you get out of Richmond. Since you're heading south, you shouldn't have any trouble."

Relieved, Eddie took off and was soon headed south toward Greensboro. Ned laid in the back seat of the plane, taking a nap so as to be refreshed for the two upcoming races in North Carolina. Sometime later, Eddie awakened him.

"Ned, the clouds are getting lower and we may have to land somewhere."

"Okay, that'll be fine," Ned replied, not alarmed at all. He lay back down and went to sleep once more.

A little while later, Eddie shook Ned awake again.

"Put your seat belt on, we're gonna have to land."

Ned sat up, fastened his seat belt and watched for the airport where they would land. He realized there was no airport and Eddie was heading toward a cornfield. Ned glanced over and saw a lespedeza field nearby. It was flat with the low growing lespedeza lying close to the ground while the corn stood six to eight-feet high. *Wonder why he's gonna land in a cornfield and not that lespedeza field?* he wondered silently. But he made no comment. As they slid into the cornfield, corn and stalks went flying in every direction. The tall stalks made a terrible noise crashing against the wings, fuselage and propellers. Ned turned and looked behind them as they raced through the rows, and mayhem followed in their path as hundreds of tall corn stalks lay crushed and shattered in their wake. They finally bounced to a stop at the edge of the cornfield just at the lip of a deep ditch. As they stopped, the nose of the plane tipped over into the ditch, leaving the tail stuck high in the air, corn hanging from the back. They had landed in Altavista, Virginia about 500 yards from Highway 29. No one had spoken during the whole event and as they crawled out of the craft and stood in the field beside it, Eddie turned to Ned.

"Goddamn, Ned, ain't you scared?"

"No," Ned answered, "you didn't tell me to be scared. You just told me to fasten my seat belt."

Ned couldn't see what all the excitement was about, but Eddie just fell to pieces right there in that cornfield. He was shaking and trembling uncontrollably.

A man from the FAA happened to be driving up 29 and witnessed the landing. He stopped to offer assistance and inspected the plane while there. The only damage he found was a small bend in the housing around one of the wheels so he told them they could take it over to the lespedeza field the next morning and fly it on out. They wouldn't be able to leave that evening because it would soon be too dark.

Ned glanced over at Eddie, curious as to whether the lespedeza field comment had made any impression on him. It hadn't. Ned never did figure out why that wasn't the field they landed in but he never mentioned it again to Eddie. The field rested right beside their landing site and was a flat site. There could have been tree stumps or anything lurking in the cornfield. The FAA official took them into the Altavista Police Department to file a report, and while there, Ned inquired about a taxi. Soon a taxi pulled up in front of the department and Ned entered it.

"Where to, buddy?" the driver asked.

"Greensboro," Ned answered.

"Greensboro?"

"Yeah, Greensboro."

"North Carolina?"

"Yeah, Greensboro, North Carolina. And try to hurry, I'm trying to make a race."

"Uh, that'll be $30, Mister." The cab driver was reluctant to start without getting an understanding about payment from his fare. He didn't want to be stiffed on such a long trip.

Ned reached into his wallet and pulled out two 20s.

"Just keep that as your tip if you get me there in a hurry."

Ned arrived in Greensboro in record time but he still missed the first race. Undeterred, he sat patiently waiting for the second one to start. Soon, he was behind the wheel of his own car that had been driven there by another friend and he was ready to race. He won that race with no problems, collected his winnings and headed back home to Hickory. By the time he arrived home, it was late and Martha was already asleep. As he entered their bedroom, she sat up.

"Are you okay?" she inquired sleepily.

"Yeah, I'm fine, go on back to sleep."

"How'd it go today?"

"I won two races and was in a plane crash," he explained.

"What?!" She sat straight up in bed, instantly awake.

"I'm okay," he assured her, "but it was a very eventful weekend."

On May 23, 1964, drivers from around the country descended on Charlotte, N. C. for the very popular and much acclaimed World 600 to be run the next day at the Charlotte Motor Speedway.

Ned Jarrett and Fireball Roberts found themselves sitting together beside the pool at the local Holiday Inn the night before race day. Some of the other drivers were inside partying and the two escaped for some quiet time before going to bed in preparation for the next day's race. Even by the pool, they could hear Curtis Turner laughing and yelling inside. They smiled at each other, Fireball shaking his head slightly.

"He's wound up tonight, ain't he?"

"Yeah, he'll be really wound up on the track tomorrow, I suspect," Ned remarked.

The two sat silently for a few minutes, just resting and thinking and planning for tomorrow.

"I hope everything goes well tomorrow," Ned interrupted the silence. "My car is running real good so it should be a good race."

"Yeah, mine's running good too. I'm always glad to be here, but this gets to be a longer race every year."

The World 600 was indeed the longest race sanctioned by NASCAR and could be quite grueling on the drivers. The extra 100 miles over the Darlington 500 generally took its toll, especially on more inexperienced drivers.

"This is gonna be my last year to run," Fireball announced.

"Oh, yeah? I'm sorry to hear that, Fireball. You've done a lot for the sport and you mean a lot to me and most of the other drivers."

"Thanks, Ned, but I'm just getting tired. I just think it's time to hang it up. I've got a contract to be a spokesperson for Black Label Beer and that'll keep the wolf away from the door, I figure. I'm just getting too old to be running around in circles with all those young kids. They got no fear and no sense of danger. It's been a good run for me and I have no regrets but just figure it's time to quit."

"Congratulations, Fireball, and I really mean it. You'll be successful, no matter what you decide to do, that's for sure. I just want you to know how much I respect you and how much your friendship has meant to me. We've had a lot of fun and good times and I appreciate being so close to you."

The two sat beside each other in the warm May evening, just enjoying being together, making occasional conversation, but mainly reflecting within themselves, recalling memories, good times, hard times, lost friends and personal losses.

The day dawned bright and clear on Sunday, May 24, 1964. The air was electric with excitement and anticipation around the large oval track that morning. The drivers and their crews made final checks on their cars as they waited for the fans to arrive. It was a sellout and several hours before the flag was to drop, the stands began to fill with noisy spectators, hauling in their coolers, umbrellas, hats, children, cameras and programs. Soon the aisles of the stadium would be filled with spilled popcorn, empty soda bottles, candy wrappers, hotdog trays and general mayhem created by tens of thousands of people converging into one area.

The drivers began to suit up in preparation for racing. NASCAR had a solution that was sprayed onto the uniforms or whatever a driver was wearing that would help fireproof clothing in the event of a fiery crash. It was a smelly, red solution that made the clothes stiff and uncomfortable, but it was a rule so the drivers had their clothes sprayed the day before a race. They would lay them out to dry and put them on at the last minute.

All the drivers had their clothes sprayed, with one exception. Fireball was allergic to this solution and would break out into a fearsome rash if it touched his skin. He had a statement from his doctor that he was unable to tolerate the spray so his uniform was clear of it. Fireball had a flashy, custom, tailor made uniform, unlike most of the other drivers who were wearing street clothes or even T-shirt and slacks. His uniform had zippers on the sleeves and up the legs so that it would fit snugly and not get caught on anything as he drove. It was, consequently, very difficult to get into and out of.

On one of the far turns at the track well into the race, Ned

Jarrett, Junior Johnson and Fireball Roberts were involved in a three-car pileup. Fireball's car hit a wall at an opening in the side of the track that allowed exiting into the infield from the track. Hitting the wall flipped his car over and the gas tank exploded, rupturing the firewall between the tank and the inside of the car.

The inside of his car was burning and Fireball was upside down. When he released his seat belt to try to get out, he fell into the burning gas. Ned had crawled out of his car as soon as it came to a stop since he was right side up, and he ran quickly to Fireball's car. He jerked him out of the burning car and away from the flames surrounding his head. When he got him out, Fireball screamed, "Oh, my God, help me, Ned, I'm on fire!"

The two of them struggled to get the fitted and burning uniform off him as the flames ran up the zippers from his wrists and his ankles. Ned was burned on his hands and arms as he worked with Fireball in trying to get it off but his injuries were nowhere near as bad as Fireball's. The safety people got there quickly but they had no communication with the drivers and had no idea what they were facing. Ned later told the media he didn't think Fireball would have been hurt at all if he hadn't turned over after hitting that wall. The fire had gotten into Fireball's lungs when he fell into it after releasing his seat belt. He was taken to the hospital in Charlotte and there was no burn unit at that facility.

A huge and ominous black cloud of smoke rose from the far turn, and every spectator was on their feet, staring in hushed horror as they realized that someone must have been hurt very seriously in such a crash. One of the spectators was Wade Sykes of High Point, the father of the pit crew and loyal, die-hard fan of Fireball Roberts. He stood in anguish as he waited to hear what had happened and who was hurt.

"Ladies and gentlemen, there's been a bad wreck on the far turn. We don't have any news yet as to who was involved, but we'll let you know as soon as we know. Let's bow our heads in a silent prayer for the safety of all the drivers." There was worry in the voice of the announcer.

Wade clenched his fist in tension and closed his eyes tightly. *Please, God. Please.*

When the announcement was made that Fireball, Ned and Junior had been injured and taken to the hospital, a cry went up from the crowd. Wade was devastated, but the only visible indication of his distress was his slumped shoulders. About an hour later, an update was given to the crowd, waiting anxiously and fearfully for word about the drivers they admired so much.

"Ladies and gentlemen, we've heard from the hospital. Junior Johnson wasn't injured and has been released. Ned Jarrett has burns on his hands and arms but will be okay." He hesitated and the entire crowd of fans held their breath.

"Fireball Roberts is the most seriously injured driver. He has some burns on his arms and legs and face, but he's in good hands. Let's join in a silent prayer for our brother Fireball."

Please, God. Please, Wade prayed silently and passionately.

There was only one burn unit in the country in 1964 at the time of this crash and it was in Houston, Texas. The doctors at Charlotte were in daily contact with the staff in Houston, getting instructions and advice on how to treat Fireball's burns. They talked about transferring him to Houston, but the doctors there felt it would be too risky and everything they would do for him was being accomplished in Charlotte. So Fireball stayed in Charlotte, under constant and vigilant care from a whole team of physicians and nurses.

Fireball remained in critical condition for weeks and there were daily updates on radio and TV stations as to his condition. Prayers were offered from across the nation and one heartsick fan stayed glued to the radio, listening for updates. Wade Sykes said little to anyone about his fear and concerns but kept his pain locked within his heart, his inner voice pleading for the recovery of his idol.

Fireball seemed to be getting better but the burns to his lungs were very difficult to treat. He contracted pneumonia, a common occurrence in burn victims, and soon had septicemia from the bone-deep burns on his arms and legs and the pneumonia in his lungs. Septicemia indicates that bacteria have invaded the blood and are multiplying. Pneumonia is a typical beginning to septicemia as germs in the lungs are easily washed into the blood through breathing. These bacteria release toxic products causing the heart to beat faster, increased breathing, high body temperatures and mental confusion with an eventual coma. Blood pressure drops and one by one, infected organs begin to fail and shut down. Even with treatment, more than half of the patients suffering from septicemia die each year. It is a virulent and aggressive illness, and Fireball's weakened condition coupled with the infection was just too much.

Despite the valiant efforts of doctors in Charlotte and Houston and the prayers of millions, on July 2, 1964, Fireball Roberts died from the injuries suffered in that May 24 crash. And the racing world reeled at the loss of what many considered to be the symbol of all that made racing a sport and a respected event.

Glenn "Fireball" Roberts, the man, died on July 2, 1964. But the legend never did. And neither did the contributions he made to the sport. His death was not in vain. Shortly after his death, DuPont began working on developing a new and better flame retardant so as to better protect the drivers in the event of a fiery crash. Also, the old gas tanks became obsolete, and a new fuel cell was developed by Firestone. It was placed inside the trunks of the cars and had a float in it so that gas would not spill out in a collision. A firewall was constructed around it to keep any escaping gas or flames out of the inside of a car. To this day, research and development continue on making safer gas tanks for race cars.

Wade Sykes never again attended a race. He would listen to an event on his radio at home but he would never go in person. His pain over Fireball's death was too intense and too deep. There was a race in Rockingham in 1974 and Mike approached his dad, hoping he would attend it.

"Dad, we'll just take a camper down there in the infield and just stay the whole weekend. We'll have a big time and you'll really enjoy it," Mike pleaded with his dad.

Ever since Fireball's death in 1964, Wade had refused to go to a race. When asked, he would just say, "Naw, I think I'll just hang around the house."

There would be a report on the Wide World of Sports on the radio following a race and maybe ten minutes of the race would be covered. Wade would listen to that but he had no wish to ever again attend a race in person. Mike finally did talk him into going to Rockingham that day in 1974. They watched the qualifying on Saturday and Wade was fine with it. They got up early on Sunday morning to wait for the big race and it was pouring down rain. Around 1:00 PM, the race was called because it was to rain all day long.

Mike hooked up the camper and they headed back home.

"Okay, Pop, I'll come back and get you next Saturday morning. We'll come back down here for the races."

"Okay," Wade agreed.

Mike thought about it all week, anxious to get back to Rockingham with his dad to the races. On Friday, he called Wade.

"Pop, you about ready to go in the morning?"

"Naw, I think I'm just gonna hang around the house."

Wade Sykes never went back to another racetrack. The scars of memory had been torn open by his uneventful visit to a racetrack so many years after the wreck that eventually took the life of his idol, and it was too painful for him to ignore.

CHAPTER 11
The Torch is Passed

Mike Sykes had grown up with the old race car drivers, knew their families, their children, lived, breathed and consumed racing for all of his life. It was only natural that he would take up his father's compassionate role as guardian and caretaker of the people he had known and loved since childhood.

Mike and his dad had attended the races each week, and they had drifted away from attending the events after the death of Fireball, but Mike always carried a love for the sport and the people in his heart. One day he received a call from Marvin Patch to accompany him down to Daytona for a weekend. Mike thought it would be a good weekend and Marvin had a motor coach parked there so he went down with his friend to watch the races and catch up on old times. Marvin was a driver at Indianapolis and in the stockcar races as well. The two men were sitting around talking about racing and just in-general men subjects when the conversation turned to how the Indianapolis Motor Speedway cared for, wined and dined their drivers, mechanics and owners.

"For the entire month of May, all the sponsors get together with the speedway," Marvin explained, "and take all these old drivers, mechanics, car owners, anybody associated with the events, bring them to Indianapolis and set them up in nice motels. They have two or three weeks that they entertain them. Fly them in, pay for all their expenses, take them out to eat, treat them just like royalty."

"Man, that's great!" Mike exclaimed. "I doubt if it would ever get to that level, but I wonder if somebody would do that for the stockcar drivers."

"It's worth a shot, buddy," Marvin encouraged. "Just get some of the drivers together and talk to some of the sponsors and see what you can work out. I'll be glad to get you any information you need."

So Mike left Daytona that weekend with the glimmer of an idea. There were so many of the old drivers who were having health problems and severe financial problems and there was nobody to take care of them or to speak up for them.

As soon as he got back to North Carolina, Mike called Jimmie Lewallen, Fred Harb and Tim Ferguson. They thought it was a great idea so they had a meeting in early 1991 at Mike's house.

"How we gonna do this, Mike? What's your ideas?" Jimmie inquired.

"Well, I thought I'd just write down some rules and bylaws and such about how someone can be eligible to join. I'll call a couple of the big companies and see if they would want to help us out. We can have a reunion every year and that way we can kinda keep up with where everybody is and how they're doing."

"What you gonna call it?" Fred questioned.

"How about the Old-Timer Racing Club?" Mike answered. "We can include all the old drivers, car owners, mechanics, the media that traveled with us so much of the time and even the old racing officials. Anybody who had been in racing 20 years or longer ago will be eligible. That way, we can keep getting new members all the time."

"What we gonna do besides have a reunion? Is there any other purpose?" Tim asked.

"I think we oughta help out anybody we hear about with financial or health problems. Most of these old drivers don't have health insurance and they have problems from injuries they got in racing. Seems a shame to just toss them aside and forget about them," Mike observed.

They all agreed, so the club was established as a medical foundation for any of the old timers connected with racing who might need it. Mike submitted the rules and bylaws to the state of North Carolina and had the organization declared a non-profit foundation. So it was that the Old-Timers Racing Club was formed by the seat of the pants. The organization would later become known as the Racing Legends Foundation.

Mike compiled a list of retired drivers, car owners, mechanics and media people that he could locate and sent out a letter, inviting them to the first reunion at the Moose Lodge in High Point. Many of the ones invited attended that first meeting and some had not seen each other in 20 or 30 years. They had a great time and were able to provide information on some of the group who were sick or having hard times. Mike developed a newsletter to go out quarterly, updating everyone on what was happening with some of the old-timers. It also provided an avenue for getting in touch with ones whose whereabouts were unknown as friends would call Mike and let him know addresses and circumstances of people not yet on the list. He also thought it would be a great idea to have some of the old drivers at the tracks on race day to sign autographs before the race. It would allow the fans and the young drivers an opportunity to meet and become familiar with the founding fathers of this great empire. Mike consequently contacted several large corporations for their support.

"That's a heck of an idea, Mike," Dick Beatty said.

They met in Martinsville, Virginia with a gentleman named Coach and asked his support. He listened politely.

"Well, it's a free country," he drawled. "You can do whatever you want to, but don't expect no help from NASCAR."

"I'm not asking for no help," Mike explained. "The only thing I would like to get is the old logo that was used by these drivers when they raced."

The company had adopted a new multi-color logo in the mid or late 1980s and the old, original one had not been used since. The original logo more aptly identified these early drivers than any new one as many of them had been racing before the advent of NASCAR. Some of them helped found the company as well as design the logo and it represented their roots. Mike contacted T. Wayne Robertson, who was a friend of his and an official of the company.

"Oh, yeah, that's a helluva idea, Mike. As far as I'm concerned, you can use Winston Cup insignias anywhere you want to, how you want to, whatever."

Mike got some letterheads printed using the logo and began writing to people at different racetracks with his idea of having old-time drivers there to sign autographs. About two weeks after a race in Martinsville, Mike received a letter from Daytona Beach. It was from an attorney. The letter read, in part:

> We understand you would like to use our logo, the old logo, on your letterhead. That's well and fine but there is a charge for that. The charge is $5,000 a year for the old logo, and if you want to use the multi-colored logo, it's $25,000 a year. If you should choose to use our logo without paying for it, we'll pursue it through legal channels.

That was how the letter ended.

Mike explained to the attorney that this was a very small operation with limited funds, and was a non-profit organization developed for the well-being and care of the founding fathers of racing. He further explained that there was no way that they could pay $5,000 a year, and certainly not $25,000 a year for the use of the logo. As soon as this happened, doors that had opened and applauded his idea of autograph signings were slammed shut. The names of those companies are not, to this day, revealed by Mike Sykes because of fear of retaliation from the company. Mike did receive an anonymous call from one of the companies shortly after the logo incident.

"Mike, I can't tell you who I am," the voice stated on his answering service, "but we was told to leave your organization alone, that you're bad news. I'm real sorry, man. I wish we could help you out, but we have to depend on them for our lifeblood. They got a lotta power and can do some serious damage to us. I hope you understand. It ain't nothing personal, it's just business."

Mike was visibly shaken by this turn of events and was angry over the betrayal. Bill France, Sr., had loved the old-time drivers and was always concerned with taking care of them. He was grateful to them for his success, as he knew that his company existed because of these early, rowdy men whom he looked upon as brothers. However, Bill Sr. was no longer in the picture and no longer had any influence on the company he started with the blood, sweat and tears of these early drivers. At the first reunion, Mike passed the hat and asked for donations for the drivers who were having severe medical problems. What they collected went to help defray costs of care and medication for these men. Once again, Mike approached his friend T. Wayne Robertson.

"T. Wayne, we need to establish a medical fund or something like that to help these people with their expenses."

"That's a great idea, Mike, but you're gonna have to get somebody from the company to help you out and support it."

"Well, I can probably forget that," Mike stated sadly.

"You can try anyway," T. Wayne encouraged his friend.

Mike took a deep breath and did it the proper way. He called Daytona and made an appointment with Billy France Jr. Mike had done some research and learned that the company's annual profit was over $33 million without including profits from the Daytona Speedway, Talladega Speedway, Darlington Speedway or any souvenir business. He arrived at his appointment, nervous but determined. He was escorted into France's office, reached across the wide desk and shook his hand. He noted a cool reception, but undeterred and determined to fight for this idea he believed in, he jumped in.

"Billy, I got an idea," he began, after taking a deep breath and sitting down. "It entails running a medical hardship fund for the old guys, mechanics, car owners, even the NASCAR inspectors, you know, the old media guys that's been around for umpteen years that helped make the sport what it is today. If you would put 2% of your profits from any of the last four or five years, set it over in an interest bearing savings account, this money will always remain the company's money, but the interest off of this money rolls over into an escrow account for medical hardship fund. You can use our medical group or get your own to oversee the funds. We wouldn't run out and pay their light bill or nothing like that, but I mean the bare necessities, a medical bill or something like that, that's creating a hardship. It would be great to have something like that."

Mike stopped and took a deep breath, swallowed hard, uttered a silent prayer and waited for what he hoped would not be an explosion. Billy France reared back in his chair, clasped his hands over his stomach, peered up over his glasses and sneered, "There's no way in hell that'll ever happen."

Mike sat there silently, disappointed but not surprised, not certain what move to make next.

"Is that all you needed?" France demanded brusquely.

"Yes, sir."

"Well, have a good day. Our business is finished." France got up, walked out of his office, leaving Mike sitting there. France never looked back.

Mike stood, gathered his dignity, and left the office. He would never again return to the Daytona Speedway grounds. The disappointment was bitter in his mouth as he realized that it was no longer about the people who built or died for or cared about it. It was all money. With a heavy heart, Mike Sykes left the corporate offices of the company that he had loved so well for so long. He also left his innocence and a part of his soul but not his determination and resolve to continue helping the people he cared about where and when he could. He was able to get help from many sources and people with the understanding that the company was never to know about it. The power they exert and the control they wield strike terror in the hearts of corporations and individuals who depend on this massive giant for their livelihood.

Through the years since its inception in 1991, the medical foundation has had to turn more and more to local individuals and companies for support. As the company becomes larger and more powerful, the large corporations, ever fearful of being caught helping this maverick organization, pull out, tuck tail and run.

"Bill France, Sr. would shoot somebody if he knew how the old-timers are being treated," commented one anonymous observer.

Mike Sykes remains faithful to his commitment with the Racing Legends Foundation. A reunion is held each year and funds are dispensed when and where needed as they are available. It has become a brotherhood of compassion and concern, and each year, the original group becomes smaller as someone else dies. They also, however, welcome new members as they qualify to join the organization.

CHAPTER 12
A Racing Pioneer Bids Farewell

Jimmie Lewallen began his sanctioned racing career in 1949 but had been running cars for many years prior to the birth of NASCAR. He raced motorcycles prior to cars, and ran cars for a total of 12 years. He had decided early on to opt out of a chance to be an original investor in Bill France's company, a decision he would frequently decry as his only regret and biggest mistake in his racing career. Not one to dwell on the negative and become bitter, he became a successful businessman. He worked for Vann York Auto Mall in High Point, N. C. for a total of 39 years. He was the Director of Fixed Operations, second in command under Mr. Vann York. He became a most valued and respected member of the large company and was the man everyone looked to for answers to questions or problems in any of the many divisions owned by the corporation.

In 1982, Jimmie received life-altering news. He was diagnosed with bladder cancer and was told by the medical community that he would live for a maximum of six months. The medical community, however, was not familiar with this man's strength of character and will to live. He began to fight this invader and faced the ensuing trials with the same courage and determination with which he faced all of life's battles. His stamina and survival instincts surprised and amazed everyone – except, of course, his wife and children. They not only loved this man, but they were familiar with his great spirit.

Jimmie endured 29 major surgeries, 11 rounds of chemotherapy treatment, and 7 episodes of radiation treatment through the upcoming 13 years after his 1982 diagnosis. Throughout all these struggles, he continued to work nearly everyday at Vann York Auto Mall. Once during his many years of suffering, he developed a bone infection in his leg. It was not associated with the cancer but was very debilitating. Even though walking was out of the question, his strong work ethic and responsibility were not to be deterred. He spent 3 months in Baptist Hospital in Winston Salem, fighting the infection. During his hospital stay, he conducted business on a daily basis by a telephone placed beside his bed. Doctors and nurses learned to not admonish him for working and also learned to wait patiently should they be in his room when the phone rang or while he was on the phone, talking business.

After he returned home from the hospital with the bone infection, he was still unable to walk so Mr. York bought a scooter for him and he used that daily at the auto mall. Carrie would pick him up from work, friends at work would lift him into the car and son Gary or neighbors and friends would be waiting for him to arrive home so that he could be gently removed from the car. Always believing in the power and direction of science, Jimmie would volunteer for any new type of chemotherapy being approved for use. He once subjected himself to an acid that was injected into the veins to fight the malignancy. The acid was so virulent that the veins had to be conditioned before accepting the acid so that it would not eat through the walls of the veins and kill him. A solution to accomplish this conditioning was injected first before the acid entered.

The doctors explained to the family that the pain had to be incredible with the procedure, but Jimmie didn't complain and rarely asked for pain medication. The doctors were so impressed with his strength and bravery that they asked him to counsel with other patients who were not handling their illness well. He readily agreed and would immediately call them to offer encouragement and empathy. Some of them would talk to him, some would not, but he never hesitated in his attempt to reach them and offer his shoulder. Each morning, Jimmie would get out of bed, put on a suit and tie, and report to his office, ready and able to put in a full day's work.

A new form of chemotherapy was introduced in 1995 and Jimmie willingly volunteered to give it a shot. His cancer was in remission, but he had grown tired from all the years of struggling. Many times, he would be so sick that there might have been only one bit of nourishment he could keep on his stomach. Once it was V8 juice, another time milk, and still another time lemonade. During those three or four month episodes, he would loose 40 or 50 pounds and the doctors stated that only his robust strength and size allowed him to survive these bouts. Afterwards, he would gain his weight back until the next episode. The doctors warned him that the new chemo introduced in 1995 was experimental but he wanted to try.

"It may not help me, doc," he explained as his reasoning, "but maybe it'll help somebody else down the road."

Shortly after the infusion of this new drug, Jimmie became desperately ill. He was admitted to the hospital in October 1995. His vital signs were extremely low, and the doctors stated he should have been in a deep coma. Jimmie, however, continued to talk to his family and many visitors. There were so many visitors that appointments had to be made by the hospital and there would be long lines of people waiting to greet the man they admired so much. It was not unusual for 200 people a day to visit their old friend and adversary. Not to be outdone, Jimmie went home from the hospital. On his way home, he stopped by his office and did a little work, promising to be back the following Monday.

Carrie took her man home and settled him into his favorite chair. He spent a very restless night, Carrie by his side. He finally acknowledged the next morning that he needed to go back to the hospital. On Friday, October 13, 1995, Jimmie Lewallen was returned to Baptist Hospital for his final battle. His beloved "Little Lew" Rita lived in Virginia Beach, Virginia, and came home immediately. She had been home every weekend for months to visit her parents, and she was soon by the side of his bed along with brothers Gary and Mark and mom Carrie. The doctors determined that his bowel had perforated from the chemo.

"He won't live but 4 or 5 hours," one warned the family. "I'm so sorry. We'll keep him heavily sedated with morphine and he won't feel any pain but he won't be able to communicate with you either."

Once again, the medical community underestimated this valiant man. He opened his eyes and turned to see Rita standing by him.

"Hey, Little Lew," he smiled weakly.

"Hey, Daddy, I'm here. How bad is it, Daddy?"

"Wellll, it's okay."

"Is there anything I can do for you?"

"No, I don't know of a thing. I'm just glad you're here."

They all stood by his bed, touching him, loving him, holding on. Occasionally, he would open his eyes.

"Y'all need to go get something to eat."

Once again he would close his eyes. After awhile, he would rally again.

"Ain't no need in y'all standing around my bed. Sit down and get some rest."

Carrie left the room briefly during that long weekend and Jimmie rallied when she did. He looked around as if he was making sure she was gone and then he turned to Rita.

"Do you need something, Daddy?"

"No, Sis, nothing else you can do for me but will you come back home and take care of your mama? I'm tired and I've fought this thing long enough but I need to know my girl will be here to take care of her for me."

"I'll do it, Daddy. No need to worry."

Rita knew her brothers would help as well but in the South, tradition dictates that most of the caring falls on the daughter in a family. This has been a responsibility long held, accepted and even embraced by southern families. Rita would have had it no other way.

Mr. and Mrs. York were out of state on business and Rita managed to reach them to let them know about her father's condition. They immediately flew back and arrived at Baptist Hospital on Saturday night. They entered his room and were stunned by the pallor on their friend's face. His family stood quietly by, faithfully holding his hand, wiping his lips, giving comfort as they could. Death was surely a presence in this room.

"How you doing, buddy?" Mr. York inquired.

"Hey, Boss, good to see you," he responded, smiling weakly.

Mrs. York, unable to speak, reached out and pressed his hand firmly. It felt cold and clammy to her touch but she held on, reluctant to let go. They spent awhile with Jimmie and his family, not knowing what to say, or what to do but giving comfort just by their presence and compassion. Carrie walked out with them to thank them for coming.

"Carrie, I'm so sorry. This is just terrible. Is there anything we can do?" Mr. York was shaken and distraught.

"No, Mr. York, I reckon there's not much anybody can do now but we sure do appreciate your coming by. It means a great deal to Jimmie and the whole family that he's so respected."

"He is that, I assure you, Carrie, and please call me at anytime if something happens."

"I'll do that, sir, I assure you. And thanks once again for coming by."

Carrie went back to her Jimmie, and the children left for a few minutes to go get something to eat.

"Carrie," Jimmie spoke softly. "I want you to do something for me."

"Of course, I will, Jimmie. What is it?"

"I'm afraid I'll go into a deep coma and they'll think I'm dead and I won't really be gone. Just make sure I'm gone for good before they move me. Make sure I'm cold."

She swallowed hard, cupping the face she had loved so well for so many years in her hands.

"No need to worry, Jimmie. I'll take care of it and I'll take care of you."

"I know you will. You've been a good wife."

"You're a good husband, too, Jimmie, and you've brought me much happiness. I love you."

"Love you too, girl," he smiled.

Saturday night passed slowly with Jimmie in and out of consciousness. Each time a nurse came by, she was surprised to see him still alive but no verbal comments were made to the family. The nurses whispered among themselves, however, at the unbelievable miracle in his being alive. The fact that he was still actually communicating with his loved ones, and even the nurses, when he was filled to capacity with morphine only furthered their belief that they were indeed witnessing a miracle.

Sunday dawned and the family maintained their vigil. More friends visited and he spoke briefly to a few of them.

Some he did not acknowledge at all. A nurse came in around 9 p.m. Sunday night to check his vitals.

"What is it?" Rita questioned as she took his blood pressure. Carrie, completely exhausted, had stretched out in a chair in Jimmie's room to grab a little much needed sleep.

"46 over 31," the nurse replied sadly, looking deep into Rita's eyes. "His heart rate is 35 beats a minute. I really don't know what's keeping him here."

"He's a strong man," Rita explained proudly.

"Yes, he is," the nurse agreed as she turned to leave.

At around 1:00 a.m. on Monday, October 16, 1995, Jimmie Lewallen gave up the battle. He knew when it was time to go, he knew where he was going, and he was ready. He had no doubts and no regrets. He had said his goodbyes to his family, Rita had promised to watch after his beloved Carrie, his sons would help also and he had spoken to many of his friends. Son Gary moved to his sleeping mother's side and gently awakened her.

"Mama, he's gone," he said lovingly as he held her hand.

She jumped, struggling to get out of her chair.

"Oh, no," she cried, "I should have been with him."

"No, Mama," Rita assured her, "it's okay. We were with him and it was very peaceful. He didn't wake up." The children had all thought that their father was waiting for Carrie to leave before he died. Even in death, he had tried to spare her pain.

Jimmie Lewallen was a powerful, self-controlled person who was professional up until the very end of his remarkable and successful life. Carrie was stunned and shocked by his death. She had sat by his bedside for so many years, holding his hands, loving him, praying over him and watching him come out of yet another struggle, that when the final struggle ended, she had difficulty accepting it. She crawled up into his bed and gently cradled his body in her arms, clinging to him, trying to will him alive. Gary broke down at the sight of his mother mourning for her man. As hospital personnel came in to take him away, Carrie bristled.

"No, not yet, leave him be. Don't take him yet."

The children were immediately concerned but said nothing to their mother. The hospital staff left, knowing that the family needed time with him. Rita, Gary and Mark stood by as Carrie sat by his bed, holding Jimmie's hands, raising them to her lips to kiss and brushing his hair back from his forehead. She kept her eyes glued on him, watching and listening. Officials came in about an hour later but still she wouldn't budge.

"No, not yet. Don't take him yet. I'll tell you when."

By then, the children were very uneasy.

"Mama, you need to let go. We've done all we can. He's in God's hands now," Rita explained gently to her mother.

"I know, baby, but I wanta be sure. He told me he was afraid he'd go into a deep coma and wouldn't really be gone. He wanted me to be sure he's cold before they take him away. He remembered being in that foxhole in the war and he didn't wanta be put in no hole unless he was for sure dead. And I'm gonna be sure."

They embraced their mother lovingly, sorry for their doubt and concern, and stood by her as she waited. Two hours after Jimmie Lewallen was officially declared deceased, his beloved Carrie allowed his body to be removed. She knew for certain that her Jimmie was truly gone from this earth and that she would see him once again on the other side. It was her last act of love for him.

RED DIRT TRACKS

Jimmie's funeral was held at Springfield Friends Meeting in High Point. Many strangers approached the family and told them of calls they had received from Jimmie when they were fighting cancer.

"He helped me through a real bad time," one man shared with them. "I just wanted to give up but he told me not to quit and to fight this thing. I did and I'm still here, thanks to God and Jimmie Lewallen."

The small cemetery rests just beside the church, and the mourners walked down to the burial site at the back of the cemetery. Mike Sykes was driving Jimmie's old race car in final tribute to his fallen friend. He was driving very carefully as those old cars were quite noisy. He didn't want to break the reflection and respect of the grievers. He turned off the motor and stood silently while the final words were spoken over Jimmie's coffin. Pastor Max Rees, then minister of the church, spoke quietly to Carrie, turned and walked to Mike. Mike was waiting for the mourners to leave, not wanting to shatter the dignity of the moment and their sorrow with the loud motor of the race car.

"Mike," Pastor Rees spoke as he approached, "I'd like to ask you to do something."

"Yes, sir, what is it?"

"Would you drive a lap around the cemetery with his old car? I think Jimmie would like that."

Mike was touched by the sensitivity of this man of the cloth, and was only too happy to comply. As he started the engine, the friends leaving the grounds stopped to watch. They stood in silent respect as Mike passed by. Mike slowly drove around the narrow, unpaved driveway circling the cemetery in final homage and honor to his friend. It seemed appropriate that this final run would be on a dirt driveway as Jimmie had realized so much of his success and happiness on the red dirt tracks of the racing world. His love of racing had begun on Sunday afternoons after services in this church, and it was fitting that this should be his final resting place.

CHAPTER 13
End of a Fabulous Era

Tim Ferguson enjoyed a remarkable career in racing. He is still considered one of the 50 top race drivers, and is number 11 of the greatest athletes in the state of Georgia, his home state. He was a two-time Winston Cup Champion and raced from the 1940s into the 1960s. Even after retiring from driving, he remained with the racing world. He drove the parade lap at the pre-race opening at Lowe's Motor Speedway in Charlotte before each race. Tim was fond of teasing wife Frankie by scaring her as he drove her around the track in Charlotte. He would move up within a hair's breadth of the racetrack wall.

"You're going to touch that wall!" Frankie would scream in terror.

"Don't you trust me?" Tim would ask, his eyes twinkling and a grin on his face.

"Yeah, but I know you're gonna touch that wall!" Frankie would respond.

He would laugh heartily at his frightened wife, but he never once touched that wall. The couple enjoyed his retirement and having so much time together. Tim was not bored at all and stayed busy with his furniture company and his work at the speedway. It was a whole different world from when racing had started and moonshine had been a cash product of early drivers.

Racing today is big business and young people without money or contacts within the racing world find it impossible to break into the sport, no matter how talented they may be. Sponsors want a guarantee of a sure winner or well-known personality before investing the hundreds of thousands, and sometimes millions, of dollars on an unknown driver. This fact makes the contributions made by pioneers such as Tim Ferguson even more meaningful, amazing and valuable.

In 1998, the Fergusons were presented with a crisis never before faced by this close-knit family. On January 16, 1998, Tim was diagnosed with cancer. It was rampant throughout his body, was inoperable, and doctors offered no hope of any treatment. The doctor walked slowly into the room where Tim and Frankie waited, sitting hand in hand, their shoulders pressed together. He stopped at the door, raised his eyes from Tim's chart and watched the couple briefly. The obvious love the two shared tugged at his heart. They saw him enter and both stood. Tim placed his arm around Frankie' shoulders and she slipped hers around his waist.

"No, no, sit down, you two," the doctor insisted.

He pulled a chair over and sat down in front of them, pretending to study the file. His brow was creased with a frown. Frankie felt her heart lurch and she tightened her grip on Tim's hand, as if she could ward off with her own strength what she feared. The doctor removed his glasses, cleared his throat and sighed, squirming uneasily in his chair.

"Tim, I'm so sorry but the news isn't good, I'm afraid. Your body is heavily involved with malignant tumors and I don't have any answers or much hope. Sometimes we just can't do anything, as much as we hate to admit it. This is one of those times, I'm afraid." He reached out his hand and laid it gently on Tim's knee. Frankie struggled to stifle the scream she felt rising from the depths of her soul.

"How long have I got, Doc?" Tim asked quietly.

The doctor hesitated briefly. He crossed his legs, then uncrossed them, and looked deep into Tim's eye.

"Six months maximum, Tim."

Tim's shoulders slumped and Frankie covered her mouth with her hand, afraid to breath, afraid to move for fear of losing control. Her world reeled around her and she struggled to keep from fainting. She took a deep breath to settle her nausea and turned her face to Tim, holding both his hands in hers.

"What do we need to do, doctor?" she managed to ask.

Tim had always been the head of this household, the one to whom they all turned for decisions and plans and actions and leadership. She had depended on him for over 53 years, loving him and doing all that she could to make him happy. This dedication was not a chore but had made her incredibly, deliriously happy. She had borne him 7 children, 5 of whom were still with them. She could not imagine her life without him. The very thought was alien and hateful to her. She had loved him since she was 13 years old and had been his wife since she was 16. She pulled her attention back to the present and realized the doctor was speaking to her.

"We'll make him as comfortable as possible, Frankie. There's medication we can give him to alleviate the pain."

He turned his attention to Tim.

"Do you want to be hospitalized, Tim, so we can better monitor your care and make sure you're comfortable all the time?"

"No!" Tim and Frankie spoke in unison, both sitting up straight, their eyes wide with anger and determination.

"No, Doc," Tim declared. "I'll stay at home as long as possible. Until I become too much of a burden on my family." He looked lovingly at Frankie.

She bristled immediately.

"You're never gonna be a burden to this family, Tim Ferguson. I'm going to take care of you myself."

They drove home in silence, their hands clasped, Frankie struggling to control her tears and her terror. They walked into their home and Tim pulled her into his arms. The sobs ripped and crashed through her body, pulling at her very insides, causing her muscles to quiver and spasm from the force. She cried until all her tears were gone and she was gasping for breath. Still the sobs tore at her, causing severe physical pain in her chest, head, back and stomach. Tim gently picked her up and carried her to their bedroom. He lay her lovingly on the bed, and lay down beside her, holding her close, stroking her hair. She snuggled against his chest, her ear pressed against his beating heart.

"I can't take it, Tim! I just can't take it! I can't live without you!"

"You've got to, Frankie," he pleaded. "You've just got to. I need you to be strong. The kids need you to be strong too."

A sense of deep peace and calm settled over Frankie. Perhaps it was the cleansing effect of her tears or maybe it was the plea in Tim's words, but she suddenly knew that she would get through this thing with Tim and that she would love him through every minute of it. She would be his strength and courage when his pain became too difficult to bear. She would suffer his every pain, she would comfort, she would soothe, she would do whatever necessary to help him. There would be nothing she wouldn't do to guide and comfort this man she loved so dearly as he fought his final battle.

And so she did. Her love became a near physical entity, a spiritual being, a soulful force guiding, comforting, leading and struggling. She could feel his agony. It swept through her body as surely and mercilessly as it did his. She would feel his comfort as pain would ease and cease. His breath was her breath, his heartbeat, her heartbeat. She slept when he slept and she was instantly awake when he moved.

He spoke to each of the children individually as he became more and more bedridden and weak.

"Richard, I want you to promise me you'll take care of your mother. Donald, I want you to promise me you'll take care of your mother. Peggy, I want you to promise me you'll take care of your mother. The boys will help, but it'll fall mainly on you girls. Carl, I want you to promise me you'll take care of your mother. Joy, I want you to promise me you'll take care of your mother. The boys will help, but it'll fall mainly on you girls."

Tim and Frankie drew comfort from each other through the long days and nights of his illness. His pain medication was steadily increased and his hours of consciousness and lucidity became more and more rare.

"Frankie."

"I'm here, Tim." She leaned over him and took his hand.

"When the time comes, I don't want the boys here. It's okay if the girls are here but not the boys."

"I'll take care of it, Tim," she promised.

Sunday, March 28, 1958, Tim rallied somewhat and spoke to each of his children, all gathered around his bed.

"I'm proud of all of you," he gasped hoarsely. "You've always been good kids and me and your mama are proud of all of you."

His eyes stopped on Frankie and she hurried to his side, taking his hands.

"I love you."

"I love you, too, Tim. Always have, always will."

They sat quietly by his bed and later that night, he slipped into a coma.

On Wednesday, all the children sat quietly with Frankie around their father's bed. He had not spoken since his goodbye to them on Sunday. Frankie watched him carefully, noticing a slight change in his breathing.

"Boys," she said, "Why don't y'all go on down to the

cleaners and pick up your suits? Me and the girls will be right here with your daddy."

"Maybe we oughta stay," Carl noted as he watched his father anxiously.

"No, I want you to go on down to the cleaners. They'll be closed in a little while." Their mother was insistent.

The boys reluctantly left, stopping by their daddy's side before leaving. Each touched his shoulder gently.

"We'll be back in a little while, Daddy. We're going to the cleaners. I love you." Carl leaned over and tenderly kissed his father's forehead.

Tim never awoke from his deep coma and on Wednesday, March 31, 1958, shortly after his sons left his side, Tim Ferguson peacefully slipped away. Frankie moved numbly through the maze of visitors and phone calls and food being delivered and dozens of floral arrangements lining the walls of the funeral home. She smiled and thanked people and shook hands but it was if there was an empty vessel standing there, going through the motions while she herself stood on the sidelines, screaming and crying and gnashing her teeth, tearing her hair. This couldn't be true. It couldn't be true. Tim couldn't be gone.

Frankie remained strong for her children, just as she had promised Tim that she would. Peggy and Donald had a particularly difficult time with their father's death. Each had to be supported and held up at the funeral. Peggy would later confess that she did not even remember going into the church for the funeral.

Throughout the days and weeks following her beloved's death, Frankie remained stoic and strong. She did it for Tim, she did it for the kids. Each day the children would gather at the home of their mother after their day at work, comforting her and each other, remembering all the happy times and funny happenings throughout their lives. And there had been so very many happy times! Of this they were all grateful.

"Are you okay, Mama?" Joy would question.

"I'm okay, honey, don't worry," she would reply bravely, forcing a smile.

The children worried nearly to distraction about their mother but she maintained a strong front. They would each cry as they sat in their mother's living room, holding each other and grieving over the man they had loved so much. They would stay as long as possible each night, but would eventually have to return to their own lives.

"Mama, do you want me to stay the night?" One or the other would ask this question each night as they prepared to leave.

"No, honey, really, I'm fine."

"Won't you come home and spend the night with me?" Joy pleaded.

"No, no, I want to stay here. This is home. I'm fine. Please don't worry."

She stood on the porch and watched until all their cars disappeared. She turned, went back inside the empty house and stood in the middle of the living room, her arms clasped tightly around her body. She raised her hands to her head, running them through her hair, and finally, from deep within her heart and soul, a primal scream of absolute grief and despair boiled into her throat and erupted into the now emptiness of the life she had shared with Tim Ferguson for 53 years, 4 months and 5 days.

Shortly after Tim's death, calls began coming in from organizations offering their condolences and awards in memory of him. TNN in Fontana, California, had engaged Tim to receive an award, but he did not live to accept it. Officials at TNN asked Frankie if she would consider accepting it in his memory. They offered to pay all her expenses as well as the expenses of any of her family she wished to bring.

Frankie did attend the ceremony along with daughter Joy. Frankie accepted the award on behalf of the family and in loving memory of Tim. Her first speech was presented in Novi, Michigan, where Tim was inducted into the Hall of Fame. She agreed to be there and make a speech and Joy accompanied her once again. She was nervous, still deep in grief, and had no idea of what she would say to these people who were honoring her husband in such a meaningful way. She walked confidently and proudly to the center of the stage as the hushed audience watched and waited, their hearts aching for this woman.

"Ladies and gentlemen, I am Mrs. Tim Ferguson." She spoke strongly and with great conviction.

She received a standing ovation.

CHAPTER 14
Doris Roberts and Jim Paschal, The Final Laps

Doris and Fireball Roberts were married for many years and had legions of friends but their best friends were Tim and Frankie Ferguson. During Fireball's last injury on the track and his battle for life, Frankie and Tim had been right there for Doris. Rumors regarding the demise of the Roberts' marriage had been circulating for quite sometime before Fireball's critical injuries on the racetrack at Charlotte. Always a very private person, Doris made no comments to anyone about their personal lives but spent each day at the hospital by Fireball's bed.

This refusal to comment remained intact, even after Fireball's death. For the rest of her life, she introduced herself as the widow of Fireball Roberts. She was a lady of great dignity, poise and character. She endeared herself to the old-time racers with her compassion and kindness. If someone was sick, a note would arrive from Doris. If someone was having any problems or hints of problems, a note would arrive from Doris. She had a sixth sense that made her sensitive to the problems of others without words having to be spoken to communicate those problems. She would just arrive on the scene, reach out with a gentle touch and kind word, and offer comfort wherever needed, without being asked.

During Tim Ferguson's bout with cancer, Doris provided friendship and comfort to Frankie, giving her encouragement, offering a shoulder to cry on, holding her hand and just being there through the hard days. After Tim's death, she was with Frankie through the long and difficult grieving process, sharing her pain, her anger, her fear. Frankie and Doris became as close as any two sisters and spoke daily, either by phone or in person.

When Doris was diagnosed with cancer, it was Frankie to whom she turned for strength. And Frankie was by the side of her dear friend through every step of her battle. It never occurred to her not to be by the side of Doris.

"She was with me through Tim's illness and death, and I'm going to be there for her," Frankie declared with deep conviction.

The weeks and months passed and Doris became weaker and weaker. She had always been a tiny woman and the ravages of cancer quickly reduced her to a frail and fragile frame of skin stretched over bone. Still a very private person, she would not allow her many friends to see her in that state. She feared upsetting or frightening anyone, and released bulletins regarding her condition through her beloved friend, Frankie. A carefully monitored list of allowed visitors, written by Doris, was maintained and closely followed by Frankie.

Near the end of her battle, Doris was admitted to the hospital. She had Frankie tell her friends that she would be out as soon as the pneumonia she was currently battling was healed. Doris was never to leave the hospital alive, and on May 5, 2004, at the age of 75, Doris McConnell Roberts breathed her last. With her went the story of her love for Fireball Roberts and any struggles they may had endured in their marriage. Always a faithful, loyal and loving wife, she maintained that role until the end of her remarkable life.

Doris had made all of her funeral arrangements with the help of friend Frankie, knowing that Frankie would carry out her last wishes. It was her directive that her funeral should be held on a Tuesday, regardless of when she died, so that any race drivers wishing to attend her funeral would be able to be there. Races are held on Sunday and drivers travel back to their homes on Monday after the events. Doris Roberts died on Wednesday, May 5 and true to her instructions, Frankie arranged for the funeral to be held on Tuesday, May 11, 2004, at Charity Baptist Church in Kannapolis, N.C.

One of Fireball's old race cars stood sentinel in front of the church as tribute to the lives and contributions to the world made by both Fireball and Doris. It was a reminder that they mattered and that their lives were important. Mourners attending the simple but beautiful service included Bobby and Donnie Allison, Fred Harb, Peewee Jones, J. B. Day, Billy Biscoe, Mike Sykes, Gary Lewallen, Frankie Ferguson, Bunny Turner (widow of Curtis Turner), and Gordon Purkle of Dawsonville, Ga. Purkle was instrumental in starting the Medical Fund in the Old-Timers' Racing Club. There was no representation, comment or floral tribute from NASCAR. Mike Sykes delivered a touching and moving eulogy for the woman whom he admired and respected so much.

"Doris was always a friend and always a lady," he explained. "Never one to complain about her own problems, she was always willing to help someone else with their problems. She was forever sending cards to people who were sick, or lonely, or sad and never asked anything in return. Proverbs 31, verse 10 very accurately describes Doris Roberts. 'Who can find a virtuous woman? For her price is far above rubies.' Doris Roberts was truly a virtuous woman and I'm going to miss her very much."

After a long and remarkable career in racing, Jim Paschal retired to spend more time with his family, Becky and Al. He worked part-time at Mendenhall Auction in High Point, as they auctioned off automobiles. He enjoyed being around the cars and having his hands on the engines. His soul connected directly with these pieces of machinery, and being near them gave him great joy and peace.

Jim had lost one lung to cancer years earlier and when he developed cancer in his remaining lung, he knew he was in for the battle of his life. Becky clung to his every word but allowed him his space. She supported him in his continuing to work. She also continued to work at her job in an insurance agency as money was scarce and medical bills were exorbitant. Jim, also a very private person, kept his illness to himself. He did not want to worry anyone and wanted to spend as much time with Becky and Al as he had left.

Becky attempted to contact NASCAR during the final weeks of his life. He had asked her to make the contact, as he wanted to speak to some of the officials and let them know how proud he was to have been a part of that company. There was no response from the company. In late June 2004, he entered Moses Cone Hospital in Greensboro for evaluation regarding a new treatment for his cancer. On July 5, 2004, with Becky holding his hand, James Roy Paschal, Jr., breathed his last. His funeral on July 8 at Briggs Funeral Home in Denton was attended by dozens of racing greats. His flag-draped casket was closed as hundreds filed by, paying their last respects to the man so many had admired for so long.

One elderly, unidentified gentleman walked slowly to the

casket, making his way through the long line winding around the room. He gently placed his right hand on the casket, bowed his head briefly, and nodded his head in a final farewell to his friend, an expression of calm distress in his eyes. He turned and left, making no comments to anyone in the room. To anyone witnessing this tribute, no comment was necessary.

Becky stood with Al by her side, greeting one by one, the many hundreds of visitors.

"I'm so sorry, Becky," one commented sadly.

"Thank you. I appreciate it. But I'm very blessed to have been loved by him," she assured the guest.

"And so am I," Al agreed, his arm resting warmly around his mother's shoulders.

Hundreds of floral arrangements lined the walls in several rooms of the funeral home. None bore the name of NASCAR or any of their representatives.

The scripture chosen for Jim Paschal appropriately described the man and his accomplishments. "I have fought the good fight, I have finished the race. I have kept the faith. Henceforth there is laid up for me the crown of righteousness." 2 Timothy 4:7-8

CHAPTER 15
A New Day Dawns

The pre-dawn sky over the back turn of the large, dark racetrack was bruised by the struggle of the warm May night, fighting to hold back the sun's ascent. A group appeared over the edge of the track's sideline, gliding silently to the top of the sharp curve. They were undeterred by the gateless fence surrounding this section of the track, and their movements left no disturbance in the heavily dewed grass. They stood silently, peering down across the steep turn, over the infield to the empty stadium and the noisy area in the bowels of the stadium. The night mist clung to the air, making the meager light escaping from beneath the structure nearly ethereal and pathetically weak.

Bill France; Tim, Floyd and Bob Ferguson with sister Evelyn; Jimmie Lewallen; Wade Sykes; Bill Blair; Curtis Turner; Fireball Roberts; Lee and Adam Petty; Tiny Lund; Billy and Bobby Myers; Jim Paschal; and Dale Earnhardt, a modern day, popular racer whose career was cut short on the racetrack, stood in awe at the power and wealth spread out before them.

"Impressive, ain't it?" Bill France observed, pride at the sight slipping into his voice.

"Yeah, whoda ever thought it woulda got this big," Curtis Turner marveled, shaking his head in wonder.

"Yeah, it got real big," Tim Ferguson stated, "but it's hard to explain just how big it really is. You just about have to see it to believe it. It's one of those deals of you needed to be there."

Lee Petty, standing beside his grandson, placed his arm across Adam's shoulder in understanding but made no comment.

"How 'bout you, Fireball? Did you see this coming?" Tiny Lund glanced to his right.

"Yep, I sure did. It was pretty big the last race I run. As a matter of fact, this was the track where I wrecked. It's grown some since then though. Even the name is different. And the cars sure ain't the same."

"Neither are the drivers, I imagine," commented Billy Myers. Bobby stood close beside his brother.

"You said that right," Adam agreed. "I realized that from watching Dad and Granddad, and hearing about Pop here, drive as I was growing up. It was pretty rough out there that year I was driving. It got a little close quarters at times. The cars were better but the speeds were higher. So were the pressures to win."

"Yeah," Jimmie said, "there's a whole lot more people in it than when we were racing, 'cept for you, Adam. You saw it at its biggest. We did it for the fun and the sport though. Wasn't no chance of making a million dollars back then, less'n you had a big sponsor. And they was scarce as hen's teeth."

"You reckon they ever remember us?" wondered Bill Blair.

"Doubt it," Floyd Ferguson commented.

"Some of 'em do. There's still a few of 'em around who work to keep our memory fresh," Jim Paschal assured them. "Course, it don't matter none, really. That's past and this is a whole new ball game."

RED DIRT TRACKS

They stood side by side, watching, remembering, smiling pensively. Dale Earnhardt made no comment, his thoughts on the past and his son, whom he knew would be racing here today.

A young man walked out of the garage area, looking silently at the darkness of the track. He knew it would soon be alive with the roar of engines, excitement of the crowds and the thunder of loud speakers. This was his favorite time – before a race, before the people arrived, before the drivers arrived. It gave him time to marvel and reflect on the wonder of this noisy, raucous sport he and so many others loved so much.

"Hey, Frank, whatcha doing?" Another man in a pit crew uniform stepped outside from behind him, lit up a cigarette, addressed his friend standing alone in the dark and tossed an empty Styrofoam cup at a trash barrel standing nearby.

"Oh, nothing. Just thinking."

"What about? We got work to do, man!"

"Yeah, I know...Do you ever think about the old guys who started all this and the young ones who have gone on?"

"What? Naw. Hell, man, what's wrong with you? That's weird!" He turned in disgust and went back inside the garage.

"Yeah, guess you're right," he muttered.

But I still wonder, he thought. *It musta been hard and they had to be really crazy about the sport. They didn't have shiny cars with all grades of safety equipment and fancy uniforms and multi-million dollar sponsors. Didn't even have pit crews, from what I understand. I salute you, fellows, wherever you are.* He raised his right hand to his forehead in a salute to the long-gone-but-not-forgotten heroes of racing.

The golden dawn brightened the east sky as the sun yawned and stretched, reaching over the far turn of the track. It suddenly exploded over the ridge, its rays slicing through the night's mist and chasing after the escaping darkness. The brilliant, Midas golden rays with the absence of red in the morning sky gave promise of a bright and clear day to come.

Never ceases to amaze me, he thought, *how something can explode with such power every day and still make no noise. There ought to be loud booms and cracks of thunder and cymbals and trumpets. All sorts of ruckus.*

He turned to leave, stopped, and focused his eyes at the edge of the ridge. For a moment he thought he caught the movement of figures. But there was no one there. *Just the sun,* he assured himself. He bent down and picked up the errant cup that had missed the barrel, tossed it inside and continued on into the garage area.

The group on the hill watched the young man peering through the darkness, sensing his sensitivity and compassion. As he saluted the emptiness, they returned his gesture.

"Yep, guess you're right, Adam. Some of them really do remember," Bill France smiled.

The group reluctantly turned to leave as the bright rays of sun raced across the blacktop track, while most of their memories were filled with the red dirt tracks of yesteryear. As they moved away, they slowly dissolved into the vanishing mist, back into their state of grace.

It was going to be a good day for racing at the Lowe's Motor Speedway in Charlotte.

Epilogue
Where Are They Now?

Mike Sykes continues to operate the Old Timers Club and Medical Foundation from his home in Archdale, N.C. He lives with his wife Tammy and youngest son Daniel in Tammy's old home place. He works everyday at Murrows Transfer in Thomasville and attends races on the weekends, every chance he gets. He is dedicated to showing old race cars at area events and celebrations. His devotion to this group of people is legendary, and he writes and mails a quarterly newsletter to former drivers, mechanics, owners or corporations involved in racing. He also organizes the annual Old Timers' Reunion at the High Point Moose Lodge. It's held the first weekend in November each year.

Mike sadly comments that the group of old timers gets smaller each year, as one by one, they fade away, either by death or devastating illness, and being moved to nursing homes, mere shadows of the once great sportsmen who thrilled and excited crowds for so many years.

Tax-deductible donations to the medical foundation can be made to the Racing Legends Foundation, 119 Northeast Drive, Archdale, N.C. 27263

Peewee Jones and wife Shirley live in a modest, ranch style, brick home in Clemmons, N.C. Peewee still receives occasional calls for autographed pictures and his race car is enshrined in his backyard garage, high on a platform, covered lovingly by a large, customized cover to protect it from any airborne damage. He enjoys having company and loves to sit at a patio table in the carport, a cool breeze blowing through, and talk about his enjoyment of racing so long ago. He is suffering from diabetes and heart disease, but he's just grateful for each day. And for the opportunity he had in helping to make racing such an exciting and dynamic sport. He still attends the Virginia Racers Association and the Old Timers Club. He helped with the operation of the club in years past but is unable to do much now. His heart and loyalty remain with this group, however. At the Old Timers Reunion in High Point on November 5 and 6, 2004, Peewee was awarded the Old Timer of the Year plaque for his willingness to help and assist the club, even when suffering great personal illness or pain.

Frankie Ferguson remains close to her children and faithfully maintains a garage museum with Tim's history. She rides in the parade lap at Lowe's Motor Speedway in Charlotte, just as she and Tim did for so many years after his retirement from racing. She still gives speeches and has maintained dozens of scrapbooks recording the history of Tim and racing. She receives regular requests from sports writers and TV stations seeking information about a long-ago event. She almost always is able to find what they need and readily supplies it to them. She is a great ambassador for racing.

She remained in the home she and Tim had shared, reluctant to leave after his death. The children maintained close contact with daily phone calls and weekly visits but Charlotte is a large city, and even though they lived in the same city, they were miles apart. The children were increasingly concerned about being so far away from their mother, especially if she should have an emergency. Large developments, busy highways, shopping centers and a major state university system now surrounded the beautiful home she and Tim had shared so happily.

While driving around near the South Carolina border one Sunday afternoon, she heard an advertisement on the radio about a new townhouse community being developed. She jotted down the phone number and gave them a call within the next few days. The management of the complex was more than a little surprised to hear from her as they claimed they had not yet begun advertising the development. She assured them she had indeed heard the announcement and was anxious to see what they had. She was given directions, and before very long, she found the place where she wanted to move. She would be closer to her children, she would have neighbors to whom she could relate instead of the many college students surrounding her current neighborhood, and most importantly, the home had a garage so she could continue to display Tim's museum.

So it was that in July 2004, Frankie reluctantly left the home she and Tim had so happily shared and moved into a new home just inside the South Carolina border. It was a happy move, however, as she is convinced that Tim somehow had a hand in her finding the development that was still under construction and had not yet been advertised. The management still insists that no publicity had been released regarding the homes.

In an announcement to her hundreds of friends, Frankie, in her friendly, open and eloquent manner stated "I am moving...to make new memories and to cherish and hold on to the old ones. Please stop by and help me fill my new home with friends, warmth, and love!"

It is a given that love will follow this beautiful and wonderful lady throughout her journey here on earth.

Carrie Lewallen, widow of Jimmie Lewallen, continues to live in the home in Archdale she and Jimmie shared, where they raised their three children. She recently celebrated her 80th birthday and bowls weekly, in spite of having heart disease. She still drives her own car and helps daughter Rita with a catering business. Always a wonderful cook, she makes hundreds of birthday cakes every year. As a matter of fact, she unknowingly made her own birthday cake for her surprise birthday party in 2004.

"She always complains about everybody else's cakes," Rita explained, "so we decided to just let her make one for her own party – even though she had no idea that's what it was for."

Her children managed to take her completely by surprise at the event held at Springfield Friends Meeting in High Point. She and Rita were on their way to pick strawberries and Rita asked her to stop by the church for a minute on the pretense of dropping something off for Sunday. The large hall was filled with friends and well wishers, all eager to show their love and respect for Carrie and her family. Carrie was somewhat embarrassed by her appearance and complained, "I'm dressed to go pick strawberries, not be at a party." She looked lovely. She also cooked a large pot of chili and made large mounds of potato salad for the Old Timers Reunion on November 6 in High Point. She is not one to sit still.

Rita "Little Lew" Lewallen Walker, firstborn of Jimmie and Carrie Lewallen, remains very close to her mother. She moved home from Virginia shortly after her father's death to honor a promise made to him, and has remained nearby ever since. When her mother is sick or in the hospital with her heart condition, Rita spends each night with her, either in the hospital or at Carrie's home. Rita splits her time between her mother and her own family during these times of illness. It would not occur to Rita to do any less for her mother, as well as honoring the promise made to her father.

Rita's husband Keith recently suffered a major stroke and is slowly recovering, and Rita divides her time between caring for him, caring for her business and watching over her mother. Rita's family lives in Archdale, near Carrie, and Rita's oldest daughter, Terra, is a dental hygienist and office manager for an Archdale dentist. Terra is a widow, having lost her husband two years ago to a heart attack. She lives with her two children, son Stoney who is 7 and daughter Tessa who is 3. Rita's son Chad works for the Bank of America, and he lives at home with his mom and stepfather, Keith.

Rita operates a catering business and has a widespread reputation of being an excellent cook. Her meals fill the stomach and soothe the soul. She cooks lunch for the

Archdale/Trinity Rotary Club each week, even when her husband was hospitalized with his stroke. A deep sense of responsibility and honor identify the character and personality of this remarkable woman, Rita Lewallen Walker. It is an honored family trait.

Gary Lewallen, middle child of Jimmie and Carrie, is chief of police in Archdale and also looks after his mother, as much as anyone can take care of that independent and active lady. He will frequently drop by her home, enter the back door and prepare a plate of food from the ever-present store of goodies in her kitchen. Gary, also a good cook, recently completed his college degree. He and wife, Sandy, live in Trinity, right next door to Archdale and very close to Carrie and Rita.

Gary and Sandy's oldest son, Michael, and wife, Sabrina, have two children. Trevor is 7 and Kayla is 3. Andrew is the youngest son of Gary and Sandy, and is a student at Trinity High School. He is 17 years old and works part-time at the local drug store. Gary recently underwent major surgery at the N.C. Baptist Hospital in Winston Salem, the same hospital where his father died. The surgery for colon cancer was successful, much to the relief of literally thousands of concerned friends.

Gary is a very prominent and visible force in the community, always eager to help and lend a hand whenever the opportunity presents itself. One can recognize the strength and courage of his parents' characters in him, as in Rita.

Mark Lewallen, the youngest son of Carrie and Jimmie, lives and works in Richmond, Va., with wife Tracy and their two youngest children. He has three children, Ben, Megan and Zachary. As the youngest, he had very little experience with the "race stuff" with their father as Rita and Gary did but he is still proud of his heritage and maintains close contact with his mother and siblings.

Fred Harb and wife Betty live in High Point. Fred operates

a garage in town and his reputation for helping and offering advice to those with car trouble is legendary. He is active in the Old Timers Club and enjoys remembering the glory days on the red dirt tracks of racing. Fred was presented the Good Sportsmanship Award at the 2004 Old Timers Reunion.

The Petty Family-Lee Petty raced for 16 years after the formation of NASCAR and a number of years before that 1949 formation. He became the patriarch of a racing dynasty unsurpassed as son Richard, grandson Kyle, and great-grandson Adam entered the racing world to continue the tradition of the racing Pettys. Richard remains the King of Racing with over 200 wins over a 35-year career and stands at the helm of Petty Enterprises in Level Cross, N.C. He and wife Lynda live on a beautiful estate in nearby Randleman and remain devoted to their community and to racing. Both help out with volunteer work as well as the massive project developed by racing son Kyle Petty and wife Patti. The family completed the Victory Junction Gang Camp in 2004 in memory of and tribute to the memory of Kyle and Patti's son, Adam. Adam had been racing for one year in NASCAR and had made quite an impression on the public and the racing world.

While practicing for a Busch race in Loudon, N.H. on May 12, 2000, Adam's car slammed into a wall on the track, killing the 19-year-old instantly. The family, devastated by the loss, was determined to create a project to memorialize Adam and sustain his memory. To increase the tragedy of Adam's loss, on July 7, 2000, less than two months later, 30-year-old Kenny Irwin, Jr. died on the same track in New Hampshire, compounding the racing world's grief and shock. Kenny had raced for four years before his death on that ill-fated track.

Adam had often spoken of building a camp to be utilized by disabled and terminally ill children as a respite and place of carefree fun, away from medical tests and needles and sterile hospital rooms. After his tragic death in 2000, the family filled their grief stricken days with the determination and dedication that only love can accomplish. It was their wish to build this facility as a living monument and memorial to the life and love of Adam Petty.

In fall 2004, the massive and fantastic camp was completed and dedicated in loving memory of young Adam Petty. It contains a building shaped like Adam's race car; a barn filled with horses for riding, donkeys, and other farm animals so as to educate visitors who may have never seen farm animals. There are dorms, with each guest receiving an afghan crocheted or knitted by loving hands from within the community. They take these works of love home with them as a tangible reminder of the love directed their way. There are craft classes, stages where children can sing or dance or perform as they wish, a swimming pool, and lakes for fishing. The activities offered are widespread and immense, and trained counselors work carefully with the guests throughout their brief but beautiful stay at Victory Junction.

Angel Flight, Mercy Medical Airlift out of Virginia Beach, flies the young people able to visit the camp for a week into the area, free of charge. Guests of the camp are tenderly removed from the plane upon arrival at Greensboro, N.C. and are transported to Victory Junction, where they are greeting enthusiastically by staff at the camp. They receive individual and royal treatment while camping. Race drivers appear one day each week to meet with the guests, play with them, sign autographs, and offer comfort. Drivers receive as much comfort and joy on their visits as the youthful residents of the camp.

More information on the camp may be obtained online at www.victoryjunction.org or by writing to Victory Junction Gang Camp, 311 Branson Mill Road, Randleman, N.C. 27317. Richard estimates it will take $2,000,000 a year just to operate the facility. The Petty family has created a legacy of great compassion and concern for the most helpless and deserving among us.

Bill Blair, Jr. lives with his wife, Sheila, in Thomasville, N.C. on a large, fenced-in estate "guarded" by family pet and companion Cody, a beautiful red Irish setter. Bill states he keeps moving further into the country to stay away from the city limits. He has a large, modern garage where he spends his days building engines for today's racing teams, as well as renovating old race cars. He also races in old time races whenever given the opportunity.

He is a gifted craftsman in building these engines and also retains a wealth of memories of the glory days of racing when so many of his father's friends would stop by the family farm to camp out and share stories on their way to and from the races. He counts among his role models and mentors some of the sport's greatest. His undisputed hero, however, was Jim Paschal. His heart and mind retain the wisdom and guidance of this gentle and great man of racing.

Becky Paschal, like so many of her sisters in racing before her, buried her beloved husband Jim in July 2004 with great love, devotion, respect, honor and grief. She sat by his side throughout his battle with lung cancer, clinging to every word, remembering every look, every smile. When the time came to say their final farewell, she did it with dignity, class and great poise. Her pain, however, was obvious to everyone. She continues to live in Denton, N.C. near son Al and daughter-in-law Shirley. She works for an insurance company in Greensboro but readily admits that she misses her Jimbo every minute of every day. They shared over 40 years together, not just physically, but emotionally, spiritually and psychologically. They had the same thoughts, ideals, beliefs and hopes. As is so often the case when two people have been together and loved each other for so long, their very souls become as one, and when half the couple is gone, the other is left with a void and emptiness that is never completely healed or overcome. She accepted the Bill Blair Strictly Stock Driver

Award in memory of Jim at the 2004 reunion.

Billy Biscoe lives in Denton, N.C. and still suffers the effects of a devastating stroke several years ago. He quit racing many years ago after losing his first wife, son, and home to his obsession with fast cars and a faster lifestyle. He worked for many years for Petty Enterprises, building and developing engines for them, and he operates a garage today. He still gives advice and encouragement to drivers, doing all that he can to help them succeed in their quest on the racetracks.

He is a kind, sensitive and generous man and carries with him the memories of so many of his friends who died on the dirt tracks of racing or in the jungles of Vietnam. He has no bitterness and takes responsibility for everything that has happened to him, both the good and bad. He never asks why he had a massive stroke, but is just thankful that he was given the strength to recover as well from it as he has. At the 2004 old timers reunion, he walked to the front, unaided, to accept the Old Timer of the 1970s award.

Ned Jarrett, "Gentleman Ned", as he was known in the racing world, lives in retirement with his wife, Martha, in Newton, N.C. But he does not live in obscurity. A heart patient, he remains involved and active in the sport of racing that he loves so well. He retired from racing in 1966 but remains a very popular and sought after hero of the sport. He is under contract with Coca-Cola and makes several appearances a year for them. He also makes appearances for the Ford Motor Company and his racing giant son Dale Jarrett's business, Dale Jarrett Racing Adventure.

Ned also has a daily radio program named Ned Jarrett's World of Racing through MRN radio, which advertises itself as the voice of NASCAR. His syndicated program plays on approximately 200 stations around the country. His memories, like so many of the racing greats, are good and bad, gentle and violent. But he has no regrets about the career path he chose. The joy of those memories as well as the scars they left sustain him, even today.

The death of his friend, Fireball Roberts, still lies heavy on his heart and in his mind. These people never forget each other or the impact their lives and careers have, and had, on each one.

Robert Nooe and wife, Marie, live in Archdale, N.C. Robert raced for only one year. He had married, and found it to be too expensive so he quit. Even today, he enjoys the happy memories of that year and states that he wishes he had continued.

For his 75th birthday in 2003, his family presented him with the Richard Petty Driving Experience gift at Lowe's Motor Speedway in Charlotte. He was allowed to drive a car around the racetrack for three laps and was then presented a certificate as a graduate of the Rookie Experience. He attained a speed of 132.15 MPH on that day, and said if he had been allowed to drive more laps, he could have gone faster. It was quite a thrill for this old-time racer to once again be behind the wheel and on the track, even if he wasn't actually racing.

The love of the sport becomes a part of the psyche and soul of every driver, no matter how long or how short their experience.

Today's Racing Dynasty continues

The Earnhardts – Dale Earnhardt began his racing career in 1975 and quickly gained a reputation as The Intimidator. He became a controversial but much loved figure on the nation's racetracks. He would push and shove anyone who got in his way, instigating many after-race fights with other drivers and/or crews. The fans loved him as he sped and crashed his way through a race in his black number 3 car. A no-nonsense driver, he made few apologies for his action and advised anyone who couldn't compete with him to get out of the way. He became a great champion and a media bad boy, but endeared himself to literally tens of thousands of fans. His popularity rivaled that of Elvis.

On February 18, 2002, at the age of 49, Dale Earnhardt crashed during a race at Daytona and died instantly. The death of this strong figure, this Intimidator, this idol to millions sent shock waves throughout the industry and the world.

Son Dale Earnhardt, Jr. had begun racing alongside his father in 1999. He and his father had become quite close and Dale Jr. quickly showed the same talent and courage his father possessed. He streaked up the line as a famous and favorite son of racing to the fans. He took his father's death very hard and became even more determined to carry on the legacy of racing begun by Dale Sr. He has continued to win and be a formidable force and champion in racing.

On July 18, 2004, Dale Jr. was practicing for an American Le Mans Series race in Sonoma, Ca. at the Infineon Raceway. He crashed his car and a fire broke out. He managed to escape with painful burns to his legs, but they were not, fortunately, life threatening. A couple of months after the crash, he went public with what had happened on that fateful day.

After the crash, he was struggling to get out of the burning trap. There suddenly appeared a man who pulled him out of and away from the burning vehicle. As he turned to thank him, he realized there was no one there. He agonized over this memory for sometime, absolutely convinced that it was his father who pulled him from that burning wreck. He was finally compelled to go public with his experience, not knowing what the reaction would be to this revelation. Not surprisingly, there were no criticisms or snickers from his adoring fans and public. It has long been believed that these loving and courageous people look after each other, even beyond their graves.

The year 2004 was the first time that the Winston Cup became known as the Nextel Cup. Competition for the championship was especially fierce that season, due in part to Nextel now being the sponsor and also in the changes by NASCAR in the point system. Dale Jr. was frontrunner at one point in the 2004 race for the championship and was interviewed by the media after a win. He made the controversial comment, "Winning don't mean shit," and as a punishment, 25 points were removed from his total points. He appealed the decision on the fact that he did not make the comment in anger. It was a comment of passion and glee. His appeal was denied, and he quickly fell behind in the points race for the championship.

At the end of the season, Kurt Busch was the first ever Nextel Cup Champion, against a total of 10 drivers fighting for the championship. It was an exciting, nail-biting, down-to-the-wire season with the last race in Homestead, Florida, finally determining the national champion. Dale finished fifth, down 108 points so the 25 points he lost for his controversial comment made little difference in the end. It did, however, cause the media to change their policy when conducting live interviews. They now have a 5-second delay so that any possible controversial words or comments can be edited or bleeped. Kurt Busch won $5.2 million as champion so one four letter word can be extremely expensive and career altering for any driver and their team.

Hendrick Motorsports is a success story of fairy tale proportions in the racing and business worlds. Rick Hendrick, one of the nation's largest car dealers, has been a business leader in Charlotte, N.C. for many years. He also operates a motorsports business that has become a dominant and formidable force in the racing world. Drivers for Hendrick include Jeff Gordon, Jimmie Johnson, Terry Labonte and Brian Vickers, all superstars in the sport. Son Ricky Hendrick raced for a short time for his father's company, much to the fear and concern of the senior Hendrick. After suffering injuries in a track accident, Ricky decided to quit racing and help his father in his business. A relieved Rick Hendrick welcomed this news.

Ironically, this relief did not change the course of destiny. On October 24, 2004, a tragic plane crash outside Martinsville, Va., in a plane owned by the Hendrick company, took the lives of the company's president, general manager, chief engine builder and young heir apparent, as well as six other people. Four of Rick Hendrick's close family members were lost in the fog and mist of that day on the side of a mountain.

Ricky Hendrick, 24-year-old son; John Hendrick, 53-year-old brother and company president; and John's 22-year-old twin daughters, Rick's nieces, Kimberly and Jennifer died on that mountain side. Also lost were general manager Jeff Turner; chief engine builder Randy Dorton; Joe Jackson, director of the NASCAR program at DuPont (Jeff Gordon's primary sponsor); Scott Lathram, a helicopter pilot for driver Tony Stewart; and pilots for Hendrick Motorsports Dick Tracy and Liz Morrison. The only reason Rick himself was not on the ill-fated flight was because he had been sick with the flu.

After the race at Martinsville, which driver Jimmie Johnson won, the announcement was made about the tragedy. Fans, family and other teams reeled from the news.

"It's like a hammer to the chest," Dale Jr. gasped. "It takes the wind out of you."

On Sunday, October 31, Jimmie Johnson won the Bass Pro Shops 500 race at Atlanta Motor Speedway, his third straight win. As he drove into Victory Lane, he wiped tears of emotion from his eyes.

"I had 10 angels riding with me today," he stated with deep emotion. "Maybe this will put a smile on some faces of our family at Hendrick Motorsports. I don't think they've smiled in a week."

Jimmie's cell phone rang and he answered to Rick Hendrick on the other end. Rick, at home, was very emotional and very happy. He also asked Jimmie to do something for him. Ricky Hendrick had loved to annoy his dad by turning his racing cap backward. Rick wanted Jimmie to turn his hat backward as he took the victory lap, in loving memory of Ricky. Jimmie and the whole Hendrick team were way ahead of their boss and already had their hats turned around, the bills of their caps resting on their backs. Drivers, crew members and employees all had their hats turned backward in homage to their friend and brother, Ricky Hendrick.

Manufactured By: RR Donnelley
Breinigsville, PA USA
May, 2010